ITEM

GW00731680

Please return or renew
www.hillingdon.gov.uk/renew

3 0 AUG 2013

6 – DEC 2016

2 1 ⅢⅢ 2018

WITHDRAWN

Please return by the due date stamped above. Late returns will incur
fines. Unless reserved by another reader, items can be renewed on
our website below (PIN required for online
renewals). You can also renew by
phone or in person.

HILLINGDON
LONDON

www.hillingdon.gov.uk/renew

We . . . aren't naive enough to think that we're your only source for reading about music (but if we had our way . . . watch out). For those of you who really like to know everything there is to know about an album, you'd do well to check out Continuum's "33 1/3" series of books—*Pitchfork*

For more information on the 33 1/3 series, visit 33third.blogspot.com

For a complete list of books in this series, see the back of this book

Some Girls

By Cyrus R.K. Patell

continuum

The Continuum International Publishing Group
80 Maiden Lane, New York, NY 10038
The Tower Building, 11 York Road, London SE1 7NX

www.continuumbooks.com

Copyright © 2011 by Cyrus R. K. Patell

All rights reserved. No part of this book may be reproduced,
stored in a retrieval system, or transmitted, in any form or by
any means, electronic, mechanical, photocopying, recording, or
otherwise, without the written permission of the publishers.

Library of Congress Catalogue-in-Publication Data
Patell, Cyrus R. K.
The Rolling Stones' Some girls / by Cyrus R. K. Patell.
p. cm. -- (33 1/3)
Includes bibliographical references.
ISBN 978-1-4411-9280-6 (pbk. : alk. paper) 1. Rolling Stones
Some girls. 2. Rock music--1971-1980--History and criticism. I.
Title. II. Series.

ML421.R64P36 2011
782.42166092'2--dc22   2011008354

ISBN: 978-1-4411-9280-6

Typeset by Pindar
Printed and bound in the United States of America

For
Deborah
Liam
and Caleb

Contents

Acknowledgments

I am grateful to Bryan Waterman, not only for bringing the 33 1/3 series to my attention, but also for suggesting that we propose two volumes that might work in tandem with one another as accounts of the late Seventies in New York. He and I have been collaborating for the past decade on teaching and scholarship related to our mutual interest in the history and culture of New York City, and I look forward to many more projects in the years to come. Thanks to David Barker for his faith in our vision of these two books and for his careful stewardship of a truly wonderful series. My parents, Estrella and Rusi Patell, never shared my passion for rock 'n' roll, but raised me in a household in which I learned to love music of all kinds: thanks for the records, the piano lessons, the first electric guitar, the second guitar after the first was stolen during my freshman year, and above all the love and support that I have always felt.

While researching and writing this book, I have come to realize that a host of people whom I knew "back in the day" have contributed — in large ways and small — to my understanding of the music I discuss here. Thanks to Nancy Bauer, Cabot Brown, Mary Evelyn Bruce, Andrew Cohen, Michael Cooper, Anne Corbett, Rob Gamiel, Ted Harris, Joseph Hershenson, Nicholas Jainschigg, David Kennedy, Jonathan Kolber, Kevin Leichter, Greg Lombardo, Kevin Nieves, Cynthia Penney, Ingrid Pinter, Stefan Pinter, Susan Rakov, Al Quintero, Rod Richardson, Ed Rogers, Abigail Sadler, David Ulin, Leslie Wacker, Sydney Walsh, Andy Whitney, and Richard Zabel. Some of these people continue to be close friends, while others are Facebook friends. Those who don't fall into either category are invited to drop me a line anytime.

I am grateful to my students at NYU — both graduate and undergraduate — who have helped me, over the years, to test out some of the ideas about narrative and meaning that have made their way into this book.

My greatest debts are expressed in the dedication. Liam and Caleb, two very twenty-first-century kids, had to put up with a dad who was living in the Seventies as he wrote this book and therefore wasn't able to be as present in their daily lives as he would have liked. Without the love, support, and intellectual companionship of my wife Deborah Lindsay Williams, none of the work that I do would be possible.

A Note on References

In keeping with the practice adopted by many of the books in the series, I have elected not to include either in-text references or footnotes to indicate the sources of quoted material. Interested readers can find this information at http://patell.org/books.

List of Illustrations

Chapter One – From "Honky Tonk Women" to *Some Girls*

"**W**hen I was offered the chance to make a concert film with the Stones," writes Martin Scorsese, "I knew right away that I wanted to make it in New York. For me, for many other people, they will always be a New York band."

Scorsese's remark appeared in the liner notes that accompany the soundtrack for *Shine a Light* (2008), and it made me realize that I felt the same way about the band. But, as an idea, it's counterintuitive: how could the Rolling Stones — who played a crucial role in the "British Invasion" of the Sixties — be considered "a New York band"? I started putting together a list of the Stones' most New Yorky songs and quickly realized that the list was dominated by tracks from *Some Girls* (1978).

This book takes Scorsese's remark as its point of departure. It examines *Some Girls* as a "New York album" written by a "New York band" — the Stones of the late Seventies and early Eighties. I juxtapose the history of the band with the history of the city in order to understand a crucial moment in the Stones' long career. Ultimately, this book is a case study in the roles that time and place, history and context, play in artistic production.

I've been listening to the band for 37 years now, ever since I heard "It's Only Rock 'n' Roll (But I Like It)" blaring from a car radio in the summer of 1974. It was my introduction to the Stones. It wasn't the band's most popular single ever — it only made it to 16 on the US singles chart — but something about the way it sounded — the thump of Charlie Watts's drums and the sleazy lilt of the fuzzed electric guitars overlaid with acoustic guitar strumming — had me hooked. I first heard the song while stuck in traffic with a friend and his parents on the Long Island Expressway on the way to their weekend house in Remsenburg, Long Island. The friendship didn't survive middle school, but I'm still listening to the Stones.

A few weeks later I came across the video for "It's Only Rock 'n' Roll" on Wolfman Jack's "Midnight Special," which ran on NBC from 1973 to 1981. Dressed in sailor suits, the band played the song with knowing smiles and subtle menace in a tent that slowly filled with soapsuds, as if the TV were a mouth that needed to be washed out with soap after broadcasting the Stones. I don't think I knew the word *louche* back then, but that's the word I would use now to describe the posture that the Stones were striking.

My first record player was a Panasonic combo-unit with both a turntable and a tape player. Not audiophile-worthy, but it served me well while I was in high school. The first album that I bought was the Beatles' *Sgt. Pepper's Lonely Hearts Club Band* (1967), but the second was the Stones' compilation album *Hot Rocks* (1964–1971). By the time I got to the end of Side Three — "Jumpin' Jack Flash," "Street Fighting Man," "Sympathy for the Devil," "Honky Tonk Women," "Gimme Shelter" — I knew which side of the fence I was on. Andrew Loog Oldham, whom Keith Richards describes in his autobiography, *Life* (2010), as "the great architect of the Stones' public persona," deliberately constructed a public image for the Stones that made them out to be "the anti-Beatles." Stones vs. Beatles? After Side Three of *Hot Rocks*, it was no contest as far as I was concerned. (Richard Lloyd, the guitarist for the legendary New York punk band Television, once said something similar: "When I saw the Beatles on Ed Sullivan, I thought it was interesting. Musically it was okay. But I really liked the Rolling Stones. So there were two camps: The Beatles camp and The Rolling Stones camp. So I was definitely in the Stones camp. Much darker." Television would include a cover of the "Satisfaction" in their live shows, and two different versions are preserved for posterity on *The Blow-Up and Live at the Old Waldorf*, both recorded during the band's 1978 tour.)

The song that really got me was "Honky Tonk Women." Does any song in all of rock 'n' roll have a more classic opening? The syncopated cowbell intro, the thump of Watts's bass and snare drums, and then the classic five-string open G *chunk* of Richards's chord work — it was in marked contrast to the overproduced sound of *Sgt. Pepper*, and I loved the starkness of it. In his autobiography, *Life* (2010), Richards describes learning about open G tuning and then dropping the sixth string to create a five-string sound that "cleared out the clutter" and "broke open the dam":

> With five strings you can be sparse; that's your frame, that's what you work on. "Start Me Up," "Can't You Hear Me Knocking," "Honky Tonk Women," all those leave gaps between the chords. That's what I think "Heartbreak Hotel" did to me. It was the first time I'd heard something so stark. I wasn't thinking like that in those days, but that's what hit me. It was the incredible depth, instead of everything being filled in with curlicues. To a kid of my age back then, it was startling.

"Honky Tonk Women" had the same kind of effect on me. I soon gave up classical piano and taught myself to play the electric guitar.

Years later, my wife would catch me singing a lullaby to my eldest son, who had been born a preemie at 33 weeks and 1lb. 10 oz. I was doing "kangaroo-care," holding him next to my chest with my shirt around him, and singing, very softly, "Honky Tonk Women." Not surprisingly, it was his favorite song as a toddler. I burned him a disc that featured multiple live versions of "Honky Tonk Women" in addition to the studio take, and he used to demand to watch the version of the song featured on the "Live at the Max" concert DVD (complete with gigantic inflatable honky tonk women) over and over again.

Some Girls, however, is the album with which I have had the most intense personal connection. For me, the album is indelibly associated with the death of a beloved teacher named Paul-Philippe Bolduc, who taught me French during my high school years in the late Seventies at Trinity School on New York's Upper West Side (see Figure 1.1). M. Bolduc and I had a comically contentious relationship. I was always one of the top students in my grade, and I knew that

Figure 1.1 Paul-Philippe Bolduc, mid-Seventies

he loved having me in a class, but by my junior year (1977–1978), I was acting out a little bit. I was already beginning to be a little bored with high school, I'm afraid. So when M. Bolduc wasn't calling me "Si-roose" (the French pronunciation of my first name), he was calling me "The Weasel." I know that sounds dreadful, but coming from him it really was a sign of affection.

The night before the album's release, I was at the senior prom, accompanying a friend with whom I had a non-romantic relationship. I no longer remember where it was held, though I have the image of a mid-town, East Side disco in my mind. M. Bolduc was there, accompanied by Ms. Pappas, the willowy Greek teacher of linguistics who introduced me to Latin in the fifth grade. I have a memory of them trotting onto the dance floor — "trotting" is just the word to describe M. Bolduc's lightness of step as he passed by. I don't remember seeing his lifelong partner, Frank Smith, my high school Latin teacher, in attendance: I'm pretty sure he wasn't there.

And then at some point late in the night, there was a hubbub, and a crowd was gathered on the dance floor, and our principal Mr. Hanly was telling us that we needed to leave because there'd been an accident, and word spread through the crowd that M. Bolduc had collapsed on the dance floor and needed medical attention. We went downstairs and milled anxiously on the sidewalk. And then word filtered down that my beloved French teacher was dead.

Dead.

Someone started crying. A lot of people started crying. I looked around in stunned disbelief. I ended up standing in the street with Rich, one of my friends from French class, waiting for the ambulance to arrive. After they had taken M. Bolduc away and it was clear that he really had died on the dance floor, Rich and I began to walk uptown. I'd forgotten all about my date (and she wasn't happy about it, as she let me know a few days later). We wandered up Park Avenue, mostly in silence, and I ended up staying over at Rich's house.

It was my first real encounter with death.

The next day, it was bright and sunny, and as I stood there on the sidewalk, the previous night's events seemed unreal, hallucinatory. I wasn't sure where to go. And then I remembered that the new Stones album was going on sale. So I walked down to Disc-o-Mat at Lexington and 59th Street, which had the best prices and sold new albums for $3.69. The album's packaging was striking, featuring what looked like ads for wigs on the front, with cutouts revealing faces that were actually printed on the inner sleeve (see Figure 1.2). Some of the faces on the sleeve seemed to be celebrities: I thought I could make out Marilyn Monroe, Lucille Ball, Farrah Fawcett, and Raquel Welch. Others seemed to belong to the Stones. All of the faces had bright red lipstick. On the reverse of the album's cover, the tracks were presented as if they were part of advertisements for lingerie. I couldn't wait to open it.

Carrying my new Stones disc, I took a crosstown over to Broadway, then transferred to the 104 uptown

Figure 1.2 Shrink-wrapped first pressing of *Some Girls*

(no "M" prefix yet), and on impulse got off and went to Trinity to see if there was anyone there with whom to commiserate. By the time I got home, it was evening, and I went straight to my room and cued up the disc. And when the wailing harmonic riffs of "Miss You" started coming out of my speakers, I was transported to another place and was grateful to be there. When I got to the track "Shattered," I sat in stunned silence.

I did feel shattered; I did feel like I was in tatters. And then I started to jump around, smiling. What was so great about M. Bolduc, I realized, was that he, more than anyone else I knew, embodied the idea of *joie de vivre*. He didn't love rock 'n' roll, to be sure, but he would have wanted me to start dancing again. And so I flipped over the disc, put the needle down, and did just that.

Chapter Two – The Meaning of the Stones

Shortly after the album *Black and Blue* was released, I bought a book called *The Rolling Stones: An Illustrated Record* by Roy Carr, which covered the first 14 years of the band's career. (Astounding, we all thought at the time, that a rock-and-roll band could last so long!) The book's back cover billed itself as "the first complete guide to every Rolling Stones recording with an uncompromising pictorial diary of the Stones' careers, riots *and* incredible lifestyles." It was the size of a record album, which means that it used to fit comfortably on my shelf next to *Black and Blue* and a couple of hundred albums. Now, however, the battered book with its loose pages (the glue of its "perfect" binding having long since crumbled) sticks out uncomfortably next to other oversized music and art books.

Although I count myself a fan of what's now called "classic rock," a category that increasingly — and disturbingly — seems to include bands who reached their peaks in the Eighties, I am not a vinyl fetishist. I rejoiced when I bought my first compact disc, glad to be rid of those pops and clicks that signaled the steady deterioration of vinyl albums with every play. (Think about it: hard diamond needle running in soft grooves. Just how long can a record sound pristine?) No longer would I have the shock of realizing that a beloved album would never sound the same because of a deep scratch caused by one's younger sister borrowing it — unauthorized — and allowing it to be used as a Frisbee at a party. While I'm willing to buy the argument that when first played on high-end audiophile equipment a vinyl record may sound "warmer" and therefore more "musical" than the "cold" digitized tracks on a compact disk or an audio file, I've always thought that this point of view was hopelessly elitist. To me, records quickly became a low-fi experience, and they were heavy to cart around to boot. But I digress.

Roy Carr was not a big fan of *Black and Blue*, which his book described as the band's most "nigrescent album since those bygone days when they used to perform knockabout re-spray jobs of Chuck Berry, Solomon Burke and Sam Cooke numbers." Derivative, in other words. "Of the eight extended cuts," Carr wrote, "only 'Hand of Fate' (with a nifty guitar solo from Wayne Perkins) and 'Crazy Mama' (an archetypal staggered lurch) approach the Stones' more traditional power-riff territory and even then, they are stripped to the bare essentials." And then, in a stark, single-sentence paragraph, Carr writes: "'Fool to Cry' will forever remain a subject of heated controversy." I always took that to be an indictment of Jagger's falsetto vocals: "Ooooh, Daddy you're a fool to cry." What's Jagger doing singing a tender song about a father and daughter, and ventriloquizing the voice of the daughter to boot? These are *The Rolling Stones* after all: they sing about honky tonk women and brown sugar and sympathy for the devil, usually in a lascivious drawl full of nobly slurred double-entendres.

Carr's remark suggests that there's a certain sound that a Stones' song is supposed to have. Songs like "Honky Tonk Women," "Brown Sugar," and "Sympathy for the Devil" — already iconic when *Black and Blue* was released — create a set of expectations for all later tracks by the band. They create what literary critics sometimes refer to as a "horizon of expectations." And this horizon profoundly affects the ways in which readers and listeners construct the meaning of the texts and songs that they encounter.

Let's explore this idea in more detail. By trade I am a cultural historian and a university professor. I did my doctorate in English and American Literature and Language, and I usually begin my introductory classes in literary study by asking students where they think the "meaning" of a text can be found. Many beginning students think that the meaning sits on the surface of the text and that a reader should be able to read a text once and "get it." Other students — slightly more sophisticated — believe that there's another meaning beneath the surface meaning and that by virtue of being literature majors they're receiving the equivalent of a decoder ring: they'll be able to uncover the "hidden" meaning of the text.

Both models of reading share an assumption: that meaning is primarily something that an author puts into a text. It's a function of the author's intention. So then I ask the students to think about plays. An author like Shakespeare writes a play such as *Hamlet*, and if you read it, you can employ either of the two models to decide on a certain set of "meanings" that Shakespeare has embedded into the play. But what happens when you see a *performance* of *Hamlet*? A performance is a collaboration: Shakespeare's text is interpreted by a director, who has certain intentions behind the staging that he decides to create, and then that staging has to be performed by actors, each of whom has his or her own interpretations and intentions, which may or may not fully accord with the director's. And then there are the contributions of costume designers, lightning designers, set designers, and others, all of which play a role in the constructing the "meaning" of any given performance of the play. Clearly, theater is a collaborative form in which the creation of meaning is a complex phenomenon.

And then I ask the students to apply that model to any literary text that they encounter. I ask them to understand meaning as the result of a conversation between writer and reader through the medium of the text.

This insight into the creation of meaning comes from branches of literary study known as "reader-response theory" and "reception aesthetics." In particular, a literary historian named Hans Robert Jauss suggested that every new text is greeted by a particular "horizon of expectations," which is created both by current social practices — what Jauss describes as "the milieu, views and ideology of [the] audience" — and by literary tradition. Jauss argues that

> A literary work, even when it appears to be new, does not present itself as something absolutely new in an informational vacuum, but predisposes its audience to a very specific kind of reception by announcements, overt and covert signals, familiar characteristics, or implicit allusions. It awakens memories of that which was already read, brings the reader to a specific emotional attitude, and with its beginning arouses expectations for the "middle and end," which can then be maintained intact or altered, reoriented, or even fulfilled ironically in the course of the reading according to specific rules of the genre or type of text . . . The new text evokes for the reader (listener) the horizon of expectations and rules familiar from earlier texts, which are then varied, corrected, altered, or even just reproduced.

Jauss's insight suggests that the meaning of a literary text is the result not only of its author's intention in writing it, but also of the milieu into which it is received, which includes its reader's social, cultural, historical, aesthetic, and personal contexts.

This model of literary production clearly applies to rock 'n' roll artists as well. Writers create texts and musicians create songs suspecting that they are likely to be received in a certain way by their prospective audiences. They can create art that aims to be "popular" by meeting the expectations of its audience. Or they can produce avant-garde art that aims not to be "popular" but to appeal to a limited few: the cognoscenti. Avant-garde art ignores the horizon of expectations for popular art, but it cannot evade horizons of expectations altogether: it simply meets the expectations for "avant-garde" art. And sometimes a writer or musician will issue a challenge to a particular horizon of expectations — whether it be "popular" or "avant-garde" — seeking to change that horizon but running the risk of being rejected by the audience, his or her art misunderstood or unappreciated.

The thing to remember about horizons of expectations is that they aren't stable: at both the personal and cultural levels, they shift over time. So what once seemed to be a radical departure from the norm can become the new norm. What once seemed subversive can come to seem "classic."

Where do you hear the Stones these days if you're looking for them on the radio? Most likely on "classic rock" stations. Their critics suggest that they no longer produce music that "matters" and that when they tour they are simply an oldies band.

Once upon a time, however — back in the Sixties — the Stones were a band that "mattered" because they challenged the horizon of expectations for popular music and openly rebelled against norms for acceptable behavior — and they became enormously popular doing so.

Musically, the source of the Stones' challenge to the horizon of expectations was the band's relationship to black music. Mick Jagger once told Jonathan Cott of *Rolling Stone* magazine that "music is one of the things that changes society. That old idea of not letting white children listen to black music is *true*, 'cause if you want white children to remain what they are, they mustn't." Listening to black music, Jagger said, means that "you get different attitudes to things . . . even the way you walk . . . and the way you talk." Remembering "the Twenties when jazz in Europe . . . made profound changes in that society." Slightly embarrassed by what must have seemed to him like pontificating, Jagger continued, "This sounds awfully serious!"

Jagger, however, was on to something important about what made the Stones the Stones. He and Richards had first come together because they shared a love of American black music. In his autobiography, Richards quotes a letter that he wrote to his aunt at the age of 15, describing his fateful re-encounter with Jagger on a train:

> You know I was keen on Chuck Berry and I thought I was the only fan for miles but one mornin' on Dartford Stn . . . . I was holding one of Chuck's records when a guy I knew at primary school 7–11 yrs y'know came up

to me. He's got every record Chuck Berry ever made and all his mates have too, they are all rhythm and blues fans, real R & B I mean (not this Dinah Shore, Brook Benton crap) Jimmy Reed, Muddy Waters, Chuck, Howlin' Wolf, John Lee Hooker all the Chicago bluesmen real lowdown stuff, marvelous. Bo Diddley he's another great. Anyways this guy on the station, he is called Mick Jagger [and he] is the greatest R&B singer this side of the Atlantic and I don't mean maybe.

Describing the Stones' performances at the El Mocambo Club in Toronto in the spring before they would record *Some Girls*, journalist Chet Flippo wrote that "the Stones fully reverted to what they actually were in the beginning: English schoolboys faithfully aping American Southern blues singers. If there were any way to get temporary skin transplants, these Limey boys would be black every night onstage."

One way to understand the Stones' music is to think about it through the lens of the model of culture proposed by the English cultural critic Raymond Williams, who was once praised by rock critic Robert Christgau for making "more sense than anyone about the conjunction between art and society."

Williams characterized culture as a constant struggle for dominance in which a hegemonic mainstream seeks to defuse the challenges posed to it by both *residual* and *emergent* cultural forms. According to Williams, residual culture consists of those practices that are based on the "residue of . . . some previous social and cultural institution or formation," but continue to play a role in the present, while emergent culture serves as the site or set of sites where "new meanings and values, new practices, new relationships and kinds of relationships are continually being created." Both residual and emergent cultural forms can only be recognized and indeed conceived in relation to the dominant: each represents a form of negotiation between the margin and the center over the right to control meanings, values, and practices.

It's important to realize that this description does not mean that residual cultures should be considered "unimportant" or "minor." On the contrary, they are major parts of any cultural formation. Emergent cultures are powerful, too, but on the other end of the spectrum. Williams characterized emergent culture as the site or set of sites where "new meanings and values new practices, new relationships and kinds of relationships are continually being created." Moreover, he argued, "since we are always considering relations within a cultural process, definitions of the emergent, as of the residual, can be made only in relation to a full sense of the dominant." In other words, it makes no sense to think of the emergent apart from the dominant: the very definition, or self-definition, of the emergent depends on the existence of a dominant culture.

This model of cultural interaction offers a way of conceptualizing the Stones' music as the group emerged out of the British and American pop scenes of the early Sixties, gained for itself the moniker of "World's Greatest Rock 'n' Roll Band," and then found itself regarded as a bunch of old farts by the end of the Seventies.

The band's name was taken from Muddy Waters's song "Rollin' Stone," a sudden inspiration when the band was pressed to give its name to a club owner before its first gig. Waters had begun recording in the late 1940s for Chess Records, playing electrified Delta blues, and by 1950 he had become the most popular bluesman in Chicago. "Rollin' Stone" itself was an appropriation of an old Delta blues song called "Catfish Blues," and its words seemed to predict the rise of bands like the Stones: "a boy child coming, gonna be a rollin' stone, gonna be a rollin' stone." By 1955, Muddy Waters was the king of the blues, though by that time he'd developed a rivalry with Howlin' Wolf, who had actually lived with Waters after arriving in Chicago from Mississippi two years earlier. In 1955, Chess Records released a record by Otha Ellas Bates McDaniel, who was known on the Chicago streets as "Mac" and had begun making a name for himself by playing songs that featured tremolo guitar and maracas, played at a faster pace and with more swing than a typical Waters song. The Chess brothers gave Mac a new name — "Bo Diddley" after the homemade slide guitar popular among impoverished Delta musicians — and his eponymous first single was a huge radio hit.

But of all the Chess artists, it was Chuck Berry who would prove to be the biggest influence on the early Rolling Stones. Describing the band that he was in with Mick Jagger, Richards told his aunt,

> I play guitar (electric) Chuck style we got us a bass player and drummer and rhythm-guitar and we practice 2 or 3 nights a week. SWINGIN.' . . . Everything here is just fine. I just can lay off Chuck Berry though, I recently got an LP of his straight from Chess Records Chicago cost me less than an English record.

It was Jagger who had shown him how to order directly from the label.

The English blues scene itself was an example of the dynamics of dominant and emergent cultures. As Richards tells it, "The real blues purists were very stuffy and conservative, full of disapproval, nerds with glasses deciding what's really blues and what ain't." Waters's electric blues was an emergent practice, challenging a dominant orthodoxy, and when he first played in England in 1956, he followed up the expected acoustic Delta blues set with a set featuring "an electric band. And they virtually booed him off the stage. He plowed through them like a tank, as Dylan did a year or so later at the Manchester Free Trade Hall." Richards remembers that "it was hostile — and that's when I realized that people were not really listening to the music, they just wanted to be part of this wised up enclave."

By 1956, however, the blues themselves were being challenged by another emergent practice: the rock 'n' roll of Bill Haley, whose song "Rock Around the Clock" from the movie *Blackboard Jungle* was a big hit in England, and sparked a vogue for other American rock 'n' rollers such as Eddie Cochran, Jerry Lee

Lewis, Little Richard, and Elvis Presley. Richards remembers hearing Presley's "Heartbreak Hotel" for the first time:

> I think the first record I bought was Little Richard's "Long Tall Sally." Fantastic Record, even to this day. Good records just get better with age. But the one that really turned me on, like an explosion one night, listening to Radio Luxembourg on my little radio when I was supposed to be in bed and asleep, was "Heartbreak Hotel." That was the stunner. I'd never heard it before, or anything like it. I'd never heard of Elvis before. It was almost as if I'd been waiting for it to happen. When I woke up the next day I was a different guy. Suddenly I was getting overwhelmed: Buddy Holly, Eddie Cochran, Little Richard, Fats.

What "Heartbreak Hotel" gave Richards was a new way of conceiving how pop songs worked:

> It was a totally different way of delivering a song, a totally different sound, stripped down, burnt, no bullshit, no violins and ladies' choruses and schmaltz, totally different. It was bare, right to the roots that you had a feeling were there but you hadn't yet heard. I've got to take my hat off to Elvis for that. The silence is your canvas, that's your frame, that's what you work on; don't try to deafen it out. That's what "Heartbreak Hotel" did to me. It was the first time I'd heard something so stark.

It's worth remembering, too, that Richards's first public performance was with a country and western band formed by one of his schoolmates. Ultimately, the Stones would appropriate the blues of Muddy Waters, the blues rock of Chuck Berry, the rock 'n' roll of Elvis Presley, and a dollop of country and western, combining all of these forms into the distinctive sound that would begin to emerge with "Satisfaction" in 1965.

The Beatles, however, would be the ones to achieve stardom first, arriving seemingly out of nowhere in 1962, northern interlopers from Liverpool, with a hit single in "Love Me Do." Their "Mersey" sound wasn't immediately welcomed when they arrived in London in 1963, and their new "Fab Four" look — matching suits and boots instead of leather jackets, long, mop-top hairdos instead of Elvis-style pompadours — offered a challenge to the expectations of the London pop scene. But if they arrived as practitioners of an emergent form, they soon became the dominant center, once their second single, "Please Please Me," proved to be a big hit.

Now it was the Stones who were forced to come up with something new, to find a set of emergent practices that could enable them to distinguish themselves from the Beatles. They soon discovered a formula for success, with the assistance of a young man named Andrew Loog Oldham, who had been working as a publicist for the Beatles, but was fired after a dispute with Beatles manager Brian Epstein. Oldham heard the Stones play a pub in Richmond, after which (according to Richards) "things began to move with devastating speed." Oldham took advantage of his connection to the Beatles by having John Lennon and Paul McCartney visit the Stones in the studio. During the session, Lennon and McCartney completed "I Wanna Be Your Man," a song that McCartney had begun writing. The song, which was recorded by both bands, would become the Stones' second single, released on November 1, 1963, a few weeks before the Beatles' version.

Jagger and Richards were impressed enough by watching the Beatles compose a song that they followed Oldham's advice to begin writing themselves. According to Richards, the band had previously thought of songwriting as "a foreign job that somebody else did . . . But Andrew was persistent." One of the legendary moments in the career of the Stones occurred when Oldham locked Jagger and Richards up in a kitchen in Willesden and told them not to come out until they had written a song. The result was "As Time Goes By," rechristened "As Tears Go By" by Oldham, who gave it to a 17-year-old singer named Marianne Faithfull to record as a B-side, though Decca ultimately released it as an A-side. The Stones would record it in 1965 with a string arrangement by Mike Leander, performing it along with "Satisfaction" and "19th Nervous Breakdown" during their third appearance on the *Ed Sullivan Show*.

Oldham, however, wasn't done poking and prodding the band into shape. He began to fashion them, deliberately, as the anti-Beatles. Oldham "had worked with Brian Epstein and was instrumental in creating the Beatles' image," Richards recalls in his autobiography.

"We were the instrument of his revenge on Epstein. We were the dynamite, Andy Oldham the detonator." As Stephen Davis puts it in *Old Gods Almost Dead: The 40-Year Odyssey of the Rolling Stones* (2001), "Unlike the tidy and cheeky Beatles, the sullen Rolling Stones look medieval, saw-toothed and weird like something out of time." The songs they play are "polar opposites of the familiar pop love songs of the time."

If emergent cultures are defined by their relationship to the dominant center, which involves not only antagonism, but also negotiation and inspiration, then it makes sense to think of the relationship between the Beatles and the Stones in the Sixties as a relationship between a dominant band and an emergent one. Being in the emergent position seems to have suited the Stones. In the 1989 video documentary *25 × 5: The Continuing Adventures of the Rolling Stones*, Richards says that "the Beatles kicked the doors open, and we zoomed in after them and held it open. There was the Dave Clark Five, and then there was the Searchers, and Gerry and the Pacemakers, but everyone knew they were sort of peripheral stuff. The meat of the matter was the Beatles and us. In a way it turned out to be a kind of double-act throughout the Sixties." The Beatles released *Sgt. Pepper's Lonely Hearts' Club Band* at the end of 1967; the Stones followed with the less successful psychedelic album *Their Satanic Majesties Request*. Both albums featured covers shot by the photographer Michael Cooper. The white "RSVP" cover of *Beggars Banquet* (1968) seemed to echo the cover of the Beatles' White Album, released a month earlier.

Both the Beatles and the Rolling Stones were part of a larger movement sweeping through England in the early Sixties. In *25 × 5*, Stones' publicist Tony King describes the times:

> When it really took off was about the middle of the Sixties — '65 — and I think that there were two or three glorious years . . . it was just so exciting to be part of it. You just couldn't help but have fun. If you went out on the King's Road on a Saturday afternoon, there was a sort of a shared feeling that you were in the right place at the right time. It was happening in every field: in fashion, photography, playwriting, music, and it all came to a head at the same time in London. So the Stones were a part of the whole thing. It wasn't just the music.

Watching *25 × 5* today (sadly, it's an out-of-print VHS tape that has never been released on DVD), you can see vividly how the band changes: its music, its clothes, its hairstyles, and Jagger's increasingly frenetic performance style. From the mid-Sixties to the mid-Seventies, the Stones develop and consolidate their image as the outlaws of rock 'n' roll through a series of experiences that have become iconic within the history of twentieth-century popular music: "Satisfaction" on the Ed Sullivan Show; Jagger's relationship with Marianne Faithfull and Richards's with Anita Pallenberg; the death of Brian Jones and the free concert in Hyde Park for 250,000 spectators that followed;

Altamont; *Sticky Fingers* (1971) with its zipper cover by Andy Warhol; the split with Allen Klein and the ensuing tax exile; *Exile on Main Street* (1972); and the 1972 American tour, which spawned the concert film *Ladies and Gentleman: The Rolling Stones* and Robert Frank's never-released documentary *Cocksucker Blues*. Critic Dave Marsh would call the 1972 tour one of the "benchmarks of the era."

Everyone believed that the band had peaked in 1972. The 1975 tour, for which Ronnie Wood replaced the departed Mick Taylor, started with a now-legendary promotional stunt — the band playing "Brown Sugar" on a flatbed truck rolling down New York's Fifth Avenue toward Washington Square and skipping the official press conference — but received decidedly mixed reviews. The post-*Exile* albums *Goats Head Soup* (1973), *It's Only Rock 'n' Roll* (1974), and *Black and Blue* (1976) were taken as evidence that the band's glory days were over. Writing in 1976 for the *Rolling Stone Illustrated History of Rock & Roll*, Robert Christgau described *Sticky Fingers* and *Exile on Main Street* as "the Stones' summit. It is now as long since Altamont as it was between Altamont and the Stones' recording debut, and the Stones, their halfhearted fantasies of a new cultural order long since forgotten, have found their refuge in professionalism."

And then it was 1977, the year that *Some Girls* began to take shape.

Chapter Three – A City and a Band

If you juxtapose the history of the Rolling Stones with the history of New York City, you notice that while the Stones were becoming known as "the world's greatest rock 'n' roll band," the greatest city in the US seemed to plummet in public esteem, reaching a low point with the fiscal crisis that erupted in 1975. Mick Jagger would later tell *Rolling Stone*'s Jann Wenner: "The inspiration for [*Some Girls*] was really based in New York and the ways of the town. I think that gave it an extra spur and hardness."

Jagger had moved into a four-bedroom townhouse on West 73rd Street in Manhattan in late December 1976, becoming a resident of a city that was in crisis. New York was still reeling from its near-bankruptcy the previous year, when Mayor Abe Beame was forced to ask for a bailout from the federal government lest the city default on bond payments. For years New York had been relying on municipal bonds to pay its bills, rolling over its debt and simply borrowing more when new obligations arose.

President Ford turned Beame down.

The state government in Albany worked throughout the summer of 1975 to come up with solutions, and as the crisis deepened into the fall, a delegation of 15 mayors met with Ford to warn him of the "domino effect" that would occur should New York City be allowed to default. Felix Rohatyn, the chairman of the Municipal Assistance Corporation, which had been created earlier in the year to refinance the city's short-term debt, said that "the dikes are crumbling and we are running out of fingers." New York State Governor Hugh Carey sent a cable to Ford pleading with the president to realize that New York was "part of the country."

Ford was implacable: he vowed to veto any Congressional bailout of the city, leading the *New York Daily News* to publish its now-iconic front-page headline: "Ford to City: Drop Dead" (see Figure 3.1). In late November 1975, Ford relented, suggesting to Congress that it provide $2.3 billion in federal loan guaranties on a "seasonable basis." Under the arrangement, there would be no cost to taxpayers because each year's outstanding loans would have to be repaid before new funds would be made available. In fact, the U.S. Treasury ended up making millions of dollars on the loans to the city.

Meanwhile, from December 1994 to December 1995, New York City had lost 143,000 jobs. During

Figure 3.1 New York Mayor Abe Beame holding the infamous *New York Post* front page: "Ford to City: Drop Dead." Photo by Bill Stahl Jr. (NY Daily News Archive via Getty Images). Used by permission

the summer of 1995, the mayor fired 38,000 city workers including firemen, garbage collectors, librarians, and police. Anticipating the layoffs, the police union distributed brochures at Grand Central Station, Kennedy Airport, and the Port Authority titled "Welcome to Fear City" that offered a "survival guide" to the city: tourists were advised not to leave their hotels at night and not to ride the subways at all. In sympathy with the police, 10,000 sanitation workers walked off the job, leaving garbage to rot in the summer sun.

The Stones would capture the feeling in the city during the height of the fiscal crisis in the song "Shattered": "What a mess, this town's in tatters, I've been shattered . . . Go ahead, bite the Big Apple, don't mind the maggots."

By the beginning of 1977, however, things seemed as if they might be starting to turn around for the city. The Port of New York was beginning to prosper again, remaining the busiest port in the nation with 600 ship clearings per month. Even during the crisis, the city had 172,000 taxpaying businesses, and the glut of office space in downtown Manhattan was subsiding.

When the "tall ships" sailed into New York harbor to celebrate the nation's Bicentennial in July 1976, national attention focused on the city — this time, in a positive way. The city successfully hosted the Democratic National Convention that year, and tourists began returning to the city, becoming New York's second-largest industry in 1976. That fall, the New

York Yankees, who had returned to a newly renovated Yankee Stadium, won their first pennant since 1964.

Abe Beame was feeling so optimistic that he stunned the political establishment by announcing in March 1977 that he would seek re-election. As the year unfolded, however, Beame's optimism proved to be premature: not only would he lose the Democratic primary to Ed Koch, but the city would face a set of challenges that no one could foresee.

For the Stones, 1977 began with Keith Richards in Aylesbury Crown Court in London on January 10, charged with possession of cocaine and LSD. Jagger sat in the public gallery to provide moral support. Richards pleaded not guilty. Two days later, he was cleared of the LSD charge but found guilty of cocaine possession. Judge Lawrence Verney read Richards the Riot Act:

> Keith Richard,* while in this country you must obey the laws of this country. The possession of a Class A drug is regarded in this country as a sufficiently serious offence to merit both a substantial period of imprisonment and a fine . . . but in the circumstances of this case, we do not

---

* In 1963, Keith Richards dropped the "s" in his surname at the suggestion of manager Andrew Loog Oldham, who felt that "Keith Richard" looked like a rock 'n' roll star's name. By the time *Some Girls* is released in 1977, Richards had resumed using his given name in connection with his professional career. For the sake of simplicity, I refer to the guitarist as "Keith Richards" throughout this book.

consider that a period of imprisonment is appropriate at all. This is, however, the second conviction for possession of drugs, and it would be as well for you to bear in mind that should there be a third, a court is not by any means likely to take the same view.

Richards was fined £750 and required to pay £250 in court costs. "What is on trial," Richards said at the time, "is the same thing that's always been on trial. Dear old *them* and *us*. I find this all a bit weary. I've done my stint in the fucking dock. Why don't they pick on the Sex Pistols?"

The Sex Pistols would, of course, go on to have legal troubles of their own, but in the month before the Richards trial, the Pistols had become a source of national controversy in England. The band had signed a two-year deal with EMI Records the previous October, and on December 1, 1976 they had served as a last-minute replacement for another EMI recording artist — Queen — on Thames Television's *Today* show, which was ironic given that Queen was exactly the kind of bombastic rock act that punk bands like the Pistols loathed. The Sex Pistols' obscenity-laced performance on the *Today* show had the English media up in arms the next day: "The Filth and the Fury" read the front-page headline of the *Daily Mirror,* which reported that "a pop group shocked millions of viewers last night with the filthiest language heard on British television."

The Sex Pistols had become the standard-bearers for UK punk rock, but the band owed its genesis to the New York punk scene. Their manager, Malcolm McLaren, had opened a clothing store with his girlfriend, designer Vivienne Westwood, on the King's Road in London in 1971. The store, which specialized in "Teddy Boy" styles, was called "Let It Rock," but in 1975, influenced by what he saw during his visits to New York, McLaren renamed the store "Sex" and started catering to the punk and S&M crowds. He became enamored of the style and sensibility of Richard Hell, the bassist for Television, the band that had established the New York punk scene at Hilly Kristal's club CBGB's on the Bowery. It was Hell who came up with the look that would eventually become identified with punk on both sides of the Atlantic: spiked hair and cut-up T-shirts held together with safety-pins. "Richard Hell was incredible," McLaren is quoted as saying in *Please Kill Me* (1996), the influential oral history of punk edited by Legs McNeil and Gillian McCain:

> Here was a guy all deconstructed, torn down, looking like he'd just crawled out of a drain hole, looking like he was covered in slime, looking like he hadn't slept in years, looking like he hadn't washed in years, and looking like no one gave a fuck about him.
>
> And looking like he really didn't give a fuck about you! He was this wonderful, bored, drained, scarred, dirty guy with a torn T-shirt.

McLaren took the idea of Richard Hell back with him to London, and it became the template for the

Sex Pistols: "Richard Hell was a definite, 100 percent inspiration."

Meanwhile, the New York punk scene evolved. Hell left Television because of creative differences with the band's leader, Tom Verlaine. His new band, Richard Hell & the Voidoids, released the album *Blank Generation* in the fall of 1977. The album's title track had a broad influence on US and UK punk. McLaren told "the Sex Pistols, 'Write a song like "Blank Generation," but write your own bloody version,' and their own version was 'Pretty Vacant.'" Television's celebrated album *Marquee Moon* had been released in February that year, and many rock critics would come to view the Stones as a once emergent, now dominant, but soon to be residual, force in rock music, supplanted by the emergent culture of punks like Television, the Voidoids, and Patti Smith in New York, and the Sex Pistols and the Clash in the UK.

The English punks were far more antagonistic to the Stones than their counterparts in New York. In her memoir *Just Kids* (2010), Smith recounts the story of seeing Richard Hell and Television for the first time right after attending the premiere of the Rolling Stones' concert film *Ladies and Gentlemen, The Rolling Stones* (1974) with her friend and soon-to-be collaborator Lenny Kaye. Smith would adopt a Keith Richards hairstyle, and the insouciant pose on the iconic cover of her debut album *Horses*, famously photographed by Robert Mapplethorpe, owes much to Jagger's stage persona. Television would signal their debt to the Stones by performing "Satisfaction" on tour the following year.

By 1977, the UK punk bands had come to represent the working class disaffection that had once been the province of the Rolling Stones. As Dave Marsh would later put it in *Rolling Stone* magazine, "Punk began as a movement that understood the difference between Mick Jagger singing 'Play With Fire,' with its direct antagonism of English class structure, and Mick Jagger at society dinner parties." To the punks, the Stones had sold out: "Groups like the Rolling Stones are revolting," declared the Sex Pistols' lead singer Johnny Rotten: "They have nothing to offer the kids anymore." Rotten claimed that Mick Jagger should have retired in 1965. After a report (untrue as it turned out) that the Sex Pistols had "vomited and spat their way" onto an Amsterdam-bound flight at Heathrow airport in early January, EMI dropped the band. A month later, EMI signed a deal with the Stones to handle worldwide distribution beyond North America for their next four albums, with WEA handling North American distribution. The deal was worth $14 million dollars. Jagger reportedly asked EMI, "If I go on the telly and do worse things and say more swear words than the Sex Pistols, will you sack us? Because there's no way you're going to get your money back."

The Stones, however, still owed one more record under their previous contact, a live double album. In the end, three sides of the album would come from a single show played in Paris on the night that Richards learned that his infant son Tara had been discovered dead in his crib. To fill out the album, Richards suggested recording a side of R&B and reggae classics at a small venue. Jagger booked a club in Toronto called the El Mocambo. Since Canada was part of the commonwealth, no visas were required, and because Toronto was somewhat off rock's beaten track, Jagger hoped that the band could sneak in, rehearse, hold a couple of surprise gigs, and make their recording with a minimum of trouble and no media frenzy. And it was only an hour's flight away from New York, where Jagger was still negotiating for the band's North American record deal.

But when the Stones assembled in Toronto, Richards was nowhere to be found. He was apparently holed up in his estate in West Sussex with his common-law wife, Anita Pallenberg, and their son Marlon. On February 20, the band sent Richards a telegram: "We want to play. You want to play. Where are you?" Four days later, Richards, Pallenberg, their son, and 28 pieces of luggage arrived at the Toronto airport. Richard had repaired to the first-class bathroom midway through the flight, remaining there for three hours. He apparently neglected to mention to Pallenberg that he'd stowed the burnt spoon that he'd been using to cook up some heroin in her bag. It was discovered there along with a small piece of hashish by customs inspectors. On February 28, whether because of miscommunication or malign intent, the bodyguards who would normally be stationed outside Richards's door weren't there, and the Mounties busted in. Richards had managed to acquire an ounce of heroin and five grams of cocaine after arriving in Toronto, and the Mounties discovered it all in short order. "The hard part," writes Richards's biographer Victor Bockris, "was not finding the drugs but waking Keith up." Richards was booked not just for possession but also on trafficking charges. If convicted, he would face a sentence of seven years to life.

Contrary to Jagger's hopes, the Stones were suddenly in more trouble than ever.

The media frenzy, however, was just getting started, because Margaret Trudeau, the 20-something wife of Canada's prime minister, descended on the Stones' hotel, making a spectacle of herself and greatly magnifying the attention that was already focused on Richards and the rest of the Stones.

Somehow the band managed to pull itself together for rehearsals in the first week of March and then played for two nights at the El Mocambo, which had ostensibly been booked for the week by the band April Wine. Describing the first show, Chet Flippo wrote:

> Keith looked as if he belonged in the St. Michael's Hospital emergency room. He was hollow-cheeked and unshaven, gaunt, and he was so almost translucently pale that you automatically wondered how many years it had been since Mr. Sun had shined down on him. He smiled beatifically, though — almost as if he had just gotten out of jail — as he hit the first dead note licks on his black Gibson guitar (with the design of the human skull on it)

of the tortured introduction of "Honky Tonk Women." It may have been rooted in desperation, but nonetheless, the Stones pulled out all the stops. And Keith, whose soul had been stained blacker than black many years before by the spirit that anointed the legendary Robert Johnson, glowed with internal combustion that no scientist in the western world would want to identify.

The four tracks from the gigs that would ultimately appear on the live album — "Mannish Boy," "Crackin' Up," "Little Red Rooster," and "Around and Around" — were all covers of classic blues and rock 'n' roll songs, and they were generally regarded as the album's saving graces.

On March 8, Richards appeared in Old City Hall Court; Jagger decamped for Manhattan, where he issued a press release: "Margaret Trudeau is a very attractive and nice person, but we are not having an affair." He then called the *New York Post*, which ran the headline, "From An 'Insulted' Mick":

> Rock star Mick Jagger has called the *Post* to say he and Margaret Trudeau have no romantic ties, just a "passing acquaintance for two nights." Hints to the contrary are "insulting to me and insulting to her," the lead singer of the Rolling Stones declared with an injured air . . . Chatting briefly with the *Post* outside their townhouse yesterday, the willing Mrs. Jagger said the couple had been deluged with calls about Mrs. Trudeau and Jagger. "We laughed about it. We thought it was very funny."

In fact, however, the Jaggers' marriage had been strained for a very long time and would soon be over. Jagger spent the rest of March "catching hell" from Bianca (according to Flippo) and socializing with the likes of David Bowie, Bob Dylan, Iggy Pop, and Stevie Wonder.

On April 26, 1977, a new discothèque opened at 254 West 54th Street in Manhattan. Founded by four partners — Steven Rubell, Ian Schrager, Tim Savage, and Jack Dushey — Studio 54 would quickly become the most famous, or perhaps the most notorious, nightclub in the world. Rubell was the public face of the club, known for handpicking guests from among the crowds that lined up outside the disco each night. The club was always full of celebrities. Among the celebrities who were present on opening night were Mikhail Baryshnikov, Cher, Salvador Dali, Martha Graham, Jerry Hall, Debbie Harry, Robin Leach, Liza Minnelli, Brooke Shields, the recently married Donald and Ivana Trump, Diana Vreeland — and Mick and Bianca Jagger. Both Jaggers would become regulars at the club. "Studio 54 took the escapist ethic of the disco scene to its absurd extreme," writes journalist Jonathan Mahler: "An outsize prop of the Man on the Moon shoveling a coke spoon under his nose, shirtless bus-boys in white satin gym shorts and sequined jockstraps, busty women hanging upside down from trapezes, a fifty-four-hundred-square-foot dance floor crowded with undulators, balconies crowded with fornicators — this wasn't about avoiding reality as much as it was

x

about obliterating it." Bianca Jagger held her birthday party at Studio 54 in early May: she rode a white horse and was led around the dance floor by a man and a

Figure 3.2 Bianca Jagger during her birthday party at Studio 54 in 1977. Photo by Richard Corkery (NY Daily News Archive via Getty Images). Used by permission

woman who had circus costumes painted on their naked bodies. "Sympathy for the Devil" played over the club's sound system (see Figure 3.2).

It was at Studio 54 later that month that Mick Jagger met Jerry Hall and began an affair with her. By mid-summer, it was clear to the insiders at Studio 54 and the other nightspots that Jagger frequented that the relationship was serious. In his journal entry for June 28, 1977 Andy Warhol described Jagger and Hall coming into the 21 Club:

> Then Mick in a lime suit came in with Jerry Hall. I thought things were fishy with Mick and Jerry and then the plot started to thicken. Mick was so out of it that I could tell the waiters were scared he'd pass out. His head was so far back and he was singing to himself. The top part of his body was like jelly and the bottom half was tapping 3,000 taps a minute. He was putting his sunglasses on and off. Mick started going after Vincent, but it was just a ruse, because I found out later from Fred he's really passionately in love with Jerry, and it looks like there's trouble for Bianca. Jerry was saying "I really have to go," and when Peter was going to go with her to get a cab she said, "Oh that's all right, Mick will drop me off."

Later that summer, Jagger flew to the Greek island of Hydra to try to reconcile with Bianca. They were spotted at a discothèque eating at separate tables.

The journalist Anthony Haden-Guest, wrote in *New York* magazine in June, "Now is the summer of our discothèques. And every night is party night." New York Yankees' slugger Reggie Jackson spent time at Studio 54, often in the company of Ralph Destino, the chairman of Cartier who had split up with his wife that summer. "We went to Studio 54 like it was part of the evening," Destino would recall. "It was so hot then that there would always be a throng on the sidewalk begging, trying to get in, doing anything they possibly could. But Reggie would walk through that crowd like Moses through the river. The sea would part."

Jackson had come to the Yankees from Oakland with great fanfare, but he had trouble getting along with both the team's star catcher, Thurman Munson, and its manager, Billy Martin. All of the bad blood came to a boil when the second-place Yankees played the first-place Red Sox in June. The Red Sox drew their biggest crowd in 20 years for the Saturday afternoon game on June 18, which was also being televised nationally by NBC. In the middle of the sixth inning, with the Yankees losing 7–4, Jackson failed to hustle for a ball. Manager Billy Martin made a double substitution, taking out his pitcher and replacing Jackson as well. A defensive substitution in the middle of an inning was unheard of, and Jackson was irate as he came off the field. NBC's cameras caught Martin's obscene tirade as well as the fact that he had to be physically restrained by two of his coaches. "The image that had been seared on the nation's consciousness, cour-tesy of NBC Sports, was now plastered on the sports pages across the country," writes Jonathan Mahler in

Ladies and Gentlemen, The Bronx Is Burning (2005):
"the brawny black slugger, his glasses removed and set
aside, standing chest to chest with his scrawny white
manager. Much of America grinned vindictively. *Los
Angeles Times* columnist Melvin Durslag wrote that
he expected no less. This was, after all, a team that
played in the South Bronx, 'one of the meanest places
in America.'"

The Jackson–Martin confrontation was a comparatively trivial example of New York's meanness. New
York seemed to be a place (as Jagger would later sing
in "Shattered") where the crime rate was going "up, up,
up, up, up." Spike Lee's 1999 film *The Summer of Sam*
would later dramatize the fear that gripped the city
as a result of a series of shootings that had begun the
previous year. A serial killer was on the loose, armed
with a .44 caliber gun. After the murders of Alexander
Esau and Valentina Suriani in April, police discovered
a letter near the scene, addressed to NYPD Captain
Joseph Borrelli:

> I am deeply hurt by your calling me a wemon [sic]
> hater! I am not. But I am a monster. I am the "Son of
> Sam." I am a little brat. When father Sam gets drunk he
> gets mean. He beats his family. Sometimes he ties me
> up to the back of the house. Other times he locks me
> in the garage. Sam loves to drink blood. "Go out and
> kill," commands father Sam. Behind our house some
> rest. Mostly young — raped and slaughtered — their
> blood drained — just bones now. Papa Sam keeps me
> locked in the attic too. I can't get out but I look out

the attic window and watch the world go by. I feel like an outsider. I am on a different wavelength then [sic] everybody else — programmed too [sic] kill. However, to stop me you must kill me. Attention all police: Shoot me first — shoot to kill or else keep out of my way or you will die!

The letter went on in this vein, until it was signed, "Yours in murder, Mr. Monster." The contents of the letter were not made public, but the discovery of the letter was an open secret. On May 30, *New York Post* columnist Jimmy Breslin received another letter, which began:

> Hello from the gutters of N.Y.C. which are filled with dog manure, vomit, stale wine, urine and blood. Hello from the sewers of N.Y.C. which swallow up these delicacies when they are washed away by the sweeper trucks. Hello from the cracks in the sidewalks of N.Y.C. and from the ants that dwell in these cracks and feed in the dried blood of the dead that has settled into the cracks. J.B., I'm just dropping you a line to let you know that I appreciate your interest in those recent and horrendous .44 killings. I also want to tell you that I read your column daily and I find it quite informative. Tell me Jim, what will you have for July twenty-ninth?

July 29 would be the anniversary of the first Son of Sam shooting.

When David Berkowitz was finally arrested for the shootings on August 10, he reportedly said to the arresting officers: "You got me. What took you so

long?" Berkowitz would later claim to be a member
of a Satanic cult, and though he quickly confessed to
the shootings, he would later say that he was the actual
shooter only twice, with the rest of the attacks carried
out by fellow cult members. The "Sam" mentioned
in the letters turned out to be Berkowitz's former
neighbor Sam Carr, whose black Labrador retriever,
Berkowitz claimed, was possessed by a demon that
ordered him to kill. Inside Berkowitz's apartment,
police discovered Satanic graffiti and a journal in which
Berkowitz claimed to be responsible for a large number
of arsons throughout the city.

New York, and the South Bronx in particular, suffered from an arson epidemic during the Seventies.
Time magazine reported in October 1977 that "there
were 6,776 reported arsons in New York City alone,"
noting however that it was a nationwide problem.
"Arson is a barometer of urban decay," New York
City's Deputy Chief Fire Marshal John Barracato
told the magazine. "Most city fathers are ashamed to
admit they have this problem." Mario Merola, then
Bronx District Attorney and a navigator in World War
II, added that "the destruction is reminiscent of the
bombed-out cities in Europe." Much of the arson was
financially motivated, as landlords looked for a way to
dispose of unprofitable assets. "The usual strategy,"
Time wrote, was:

> drive out tenants by cutting off the heat or water; make
> sure the fire insurance is paid up; call in a torch. In effect,

says Barracato, the landlord or businessman "literally sells his building back to the insurance company because there is nobody else who will buy it." Barracato's office is currently investigating a case in which a Brooklyn building insured for $200,000 went up in flames six minutes before its insurance policy expired.

Time noted, however, that some cases of arson were financially motivated in a different way: junkies would often set fire to buildings so that they could scavenge and sell fire-resistant fixtures. And many cases were motivated by hate or revenge. "Whatever the motive for arson," *Time* concluded, "the result is fright and despair among inner-city residents."

The most spectacular eruption of crime during the summer of 1977 occurred on the night of July 13, when a combination of lightning, improperly maintained machinery, and human error caused a total blackout in New York City. The result was an unprecedented night of looting and pillaging throughout all of the city's boroughs. The blackout lasted 25 hours, and when it was over there were some shocking numbers: 1,037 fires; 1,616 damaged or looted stores; 3,776 people arrested, in what was the largest mass arrest in the city's history. The arrests, however, ultimately made little difference in the amount of looting that took place; it was six days before all of the prisoners were arraigned. The national response was in keeping with the city's seemingly all-time low prestige. *The Washington Post* described the looting as "an indictment of the state of the city, its government, and its people." In the August 15 1977 issue of the *New Yorker*, Andy Logan wrote:

> When someone is struck down by a sudden disastrous accident from which it could take years to recover, it is customary for there to be a rallying around and an outpouring of offers of help and expressions of sympathy . . . This was not the kind of response that New York received from many quarters last month . . . Instead of comfort, what New York received in the first days after the disaster was often the punitive judgment that it had just got what it deserved considering what kind of place it was.

President Carter refused to declare the city a major disaster area, which would have given the city access to federal relief funds; according to Carter, the city didn't qualify because the blackout was not a *natural* disaster. Once again, an American president was telling New York to drop dead.

Mick Jagger, meanwhile, had crime on his mind during the summer of 1977. In July, he tried to halt the publication of a novel entitled *The Man Who Killed Mick Jagger*, which had been written by David Littlejohn, who was an associate dean at the University of California. The novel, which begins and ends at a Rolling Stones gig in 1969, tells the story of a graduate student named Ronald Harrington, who comes to believe that he is a Nietzschean *Übermensch* and decides to rebel by killing "the idol of his generation, the prancing, teasing symbol of everything that at once repulses and attracts him." Ever since the murder of Sharon Tate in 1969, Jagger had worried about his personal safety, and he feared that Littlejohn's novel might give someone ideas. In his biography of Jagger, Christopher Sandford reports that *Rolling Stone* editor Jann Wenner had advised Littlejohn, "I know Jagger . . . He's continually fantasizing and in dread of being shot and killed by some nut at a rock concert." Jagger's attempt to have the book suppressed failed.

In the middle of September, the Stones released the double album *Love You Live*. Keith Richards missed the promotional party that was held on September 14 at the Marquee Club in London, where the Stones had made their live debut in 1963. He did make it to the second promotional party, this time in New York, on September 27. On October 1, the band arrived in Paris to begin working on the album that would become *Some Girls*.

Chapter Four – The Sessions

In an interview with *The Daily Express* in September 1977, Jagger had discussed the band's plans for the immediate future: "Of course I want the band to continue. We're supposed to be touring next year. I just keep thinking about it very positively. We want to make a new album. A single. Go on the road in the spring, so I'm just going ahead and planning it." Jagger arranged for the band to record at EMI's legendary Pathé-Marconi studios in the Boulogne-Billancourt suburb of Paris and hired Chris Kimsey to be the engineer for the sessions. Kimsey had met the Stones while interning as an assistant engineer at Olympic Studios in London in the late Sixties and later worked on the album *Sticky Fingers*. More recently he had served as the recording engineer for Peter Frampton's hit double album, *Frampton Comes Alive!* (1976).

Richards would later credit Kimsey for the quality of the sound on *Some Girls*. Kimsey wanted "to get more of a live sound," believing that the band's "last few albums like *Black and Blue* and *Goats Head Soup* had sounded too clean in places, almost clinical." The room in which the Stones would record at Pathé Marconi was really just a big rehearsal space. "But," according to Kimsey, "the room had such a good sound even though the desk was only 16-track, they began to feel comfortable. It made for a more relaxed atmosphere which led to a certain spontaneity in the music." The room was cheap — "like, 200 quid a day," according to Kimsey — and he enjoyed working with the "lovely old 16-track EMI desk and recording to a Studer A80 with Dolby A at 15ips." In his autobiography, Richards remembers that "the primitive mixing desk" was "the same kind of soundboard designed by EMI for Abbey Road Studios — very humble and simple, with barely more than a treble and bass button but with phenomenal sound, which Kimsey fell in love with . . . The sound it got had clarity but dirtiness, a real funky, club feel to it that suited what we were doing."

About three weeks into the sessions, Jagger announced that it was time "to move into the real room." Kimsey was surprised: "I said, 'What do you mean? What real room?'"The room that Jagger had in mind was next door and equally big. Kimsey recalls that it had an "absolutely enormous Neve [mixing console] — you had about 70 channels in front of you and a whole sidecar to the left of the monitoring that went back another four feet. In fact, the control room was the complete opposite to the one I'd been using." But Kimsey felt that the room "sounded awful," so he convinced Richards and Jagger to let the band stay where it was: "Given the price, I don't think it took very much to talk Mick into staying. He kept asking, 'Does it sound all right in here? Does it sound all right?' and I'd say, 'Yeah, it sounds great. We're getting great results.' Thank God we stayed there."

The room was a large oblong space, with a small control room that was off-center and oddly shaped: "you couldn't fit more than four people in it. And for another, the wall slanted outwards as it went towards the door, with the desk placed at an angle to the speakers so that the left-hand speaker was closer to you than the right-hand speaker." The control room's angled front wall prevented the engineer from seeing one side of the room. So Kimsey arranged the band in a semicircle that faced the control room's window: Watts's maple Gretsch drum kit flanked by Wood and Richards on the left and Jagger's amp and Wyman's setup on the right. Keyboards, including a Steinway grand, a Wurlitzer electric piano, and a Hammond organ, were placed in front of the control room window, and Kimsey positioned screens behind each band member and between their amps. Jagger sang in the middle of the semi-circle directly in front of Watts. In effect, "each of the guys were in their own little booths without anything in front of them. That meant they could actually hear what was coming out of their amps, and I also put up a little Shure PA for them to hear Mick's vocals as well as Charlie's snare and kick." Kimsey didn't want the band to use headphones, because he was trying to create "sort of a live atmosphere," and the guitars were so loud that he needed to do something to make sure Watts's snare drum could be heard. Kimsey put a mike on the drum kit that fed into the PA along with Jagger's guide vocals and mounted the PA column, which had a small horn at the top and two bass units below, seven feet into the air. "The PA was aiming at the drums, so the snare would actually come back through the overhead mic and create this quite unique sound."

Richards and Wood used Mesa Boogie amps that were close-miked, while Wyman played a Fender Mustang base through an Ampeg Portaflex amp that was "DI'd" — connected directly to the soundboard. Richards used a Gibson Les Paul Junior, as well as his signature red and cream Fender Telecasters. Wood used a Fender Stratocaster, a handcrafted Zemaitis, a Fender B-Bender Telecaster, and a pedal steel guitar. Jagger's amp was also close-miked, as were the grand piano and the Wurlitzer. The Hammond was DI'd.

Jagger and Richards later told *ZigZag* magazine that they had decided "that we were not gonna touch the tracks any more than necessary," with "hardly any overdubs" and "only a little bit of extra rhythm here and there." As a result of this initial approach, Kimsey was quite active during the recording: "They'd be in the middle of a take, and I'd never know if it was going to be the master, so I'd try all sorts of things. As it was quite a discrete desk, I could do that kind of stuff, meaning that I'd be changing sounds during a performance that might turn out to be the master. Still, they always left me to get on with my job and never, ever mentioned anything about the sound." In the end, however, the album would include some significant overdubbing. "Shattered," for example, has seven identifiable guitar parts.

The Stones rehearsed for a month and then began to record in November. The band had decided to get back to basics, using a stripped down line-up for the first time since *Let It Bleed*. They'd elected not to use studio musicians like Billy Preston and Nicky Hopkins, whom Richards described as "clever bastards" — technically superior musicians who, he felt, sometimes led the Stones too far from their basic sound. Richards was looking forward to his new partnership with Ronnie Wood, whose style resembled that of Brian Jones rather than Mick Taylor. With Taylor in the band, the division of labor between the guitarists was primarily Taylor on lead and Richards on rhythm. With Wood, Richards hoped to get back to the tandem guitar playing that had characterized the band in its early days.

Wood would later describe *Some Girls* as "one of my favorite Rolling Stones albums out of the ones that the band has made since I've been with them. In many ways, *Some Girls* was a celebration of getting Keith back, but I was also enjoying the interplay with Mick. I was having a lot of fun hanging out with Mick and being involved in shaping up the songs, as much as with Keith. Whereas Keith was saying to me, 'Hey come over to my side a bit more, you don't want to hang with the vocalist.' I had to play the whole thing very carefully!" According to Richards, the fact that the Stones "hadn't been together for a while" meant that the they "needed to get back to our old form of writing and collaborating — doing it all on the day, there and then, composing from scratch or semi-scratch. We jumped straight in, back to our old ways with remarkable results." Although critics would later describe the album as dominated by Mick Jagger, who plays guitar on many of the tracks in addition to singing, Jagger himself insisted later on that *Some Girls* was no less a collaboration than "any other album after 1975 — and before that it's too long ago to remember." According to Jagger:

> There are songs on *Some Girls* that I more or less wrote on my own — "Miss You,""When The Whip Comes Down,""Respectable" — and songs that Keith wrote — "Beast Of Burden" — and songs we wrote together. You've got to remember, there's a song and then there's an arrangement. In a band, in the studio, everyone makes a contribution. It's very amorphous, Yes, there are songs I know I came into the studio and taught the band the tune, but at the other end of the spectrum, times when I came into the studio with absolutely nothing and in half an hour we had a song and I don't know where it came from.

Wood describes the process more simply: "Mick would have a riff or Keith would have a riff, and we would just take it from there."

Richards would recall that his guitar sound on the album was, uncharacteristically, shaped by his use of an effects box:

What a lot of *Some Girls* came down to was this little green box I used, this MXR pedal, a reverb-echo. For most of the songs on there I'm using that, and it elevated the band and gave it a different sound. In a way it came down to a little bit of technology. It was kind of like "Satisfaction," a little box. On *Some Girls* I just found a way of making that thing work, at least through all of the fast songs.

As it turned out, nine of the ten songs selected for the album would be "fast songs," with "Beast of Burden" the only ballad. Jagger later said that if it had been his decision alone, he would have left "Beast of Burden" off the album, because he wanted to have a danceable album of uptempo songs.

In retrospect, Richards would describe "a certain sense of renewal" that came about during the recording of the album:

> A lot of it was, we've got to out-punk the punks. Because they can't play, and we can. All they can do is be punks. Yes, that might have been a certain thorn in the side. The Johnny Rottens, "these fucking kids." I love every band that comes along. That's why I'm here, to encourage guys to play and get bands together. But when they're not playing anything, they're just spitting on people, now come on, we can do better than that. There was also an extra urgency because of this grim aspect of the trial and also because after all the palaver, the bust, the noise, the cleaning up, I needed to prove that there was something behind all this — some purpose to this kind of suffering. And it came together very nicely.

Richards's rejuvenation was also the result of Ronnie Wood's increasing confidence as a member of the Rolling Stones. Wood had experienced some bumpy moments onstage during the 1975 tour, but three years later he and Richards had meshed. "It was definitely a huge advantage, having toured with the band so much before making this album," Wood told *Creem* magazine shortly before the album was released. "Keith pointed it out the other day; that I'd come straight into a touring vibe. Two years of it. That's one of the reasons why I think this is the best playing I've done on record."

Richards, nevertheless, was still struggling with his addictions during the sessions, and he would occasionally absent himself for extended periods of time: "I made a damn good attempt at cleaning up in 1977 with my black box and Meg Patterson and the rest, but for a brief time it didn't stick. While working on *Some Girls*, I'd go to the john from time to time and shoot up." He insists, however, that there was in fact a "method" to his absences:

> I'd think about what I was gonna do in there. I would be in there meditating about this track that was really nice but only half finished, and where it could go and what was going wrong with it, and why we'd done twenty-five takes and were still stumbling on the same block every time. When I came out, it was "Listen, it goes a little faster, and we cut out the keyboards in the middle." And sometimes I was right, sometimes I was wrong, but it had only been, hey, forty-five minutes. Better than forty-five minutes when everybody is putting their

oar in at once — "Yeah, but what about if we do this?" Which to me is murder.

And then there were those occasional moments when Richards "would go on the nod while we were playing. Still upright, but removed from present concerns, only to pick it up a few bars on. That did waste time because the take, if there was one, would have to be scrapped."

Commenting on the album after its release, Jagger told *Rolling Stone*'s Jonathan Cott:

I think there are some good songs on our last albums, but they probably lacked direction.

On the new record, the band is much more together; they really played well during the sessions — and not only on what you hear, but also on all the stuff we did. We did so much that we didn't know what to do with all of it. We had four songs with the same uptempo idea, and I originally thought of having every song be a continuation of the other. Ian Stewart, who plays piano with us, said: "Everything seems to be in A." And I said: "Well Beethoven wrote whole symphonies in one key, so what does it fucking matter."

The band considered a several titles for the album, including "More Fast Numbers," before settling on *Some Girls*. When asked why, Keith Richards is reputed to have said, "Because we couldn't remember their fucking names."

Chapter Five – The Album

Even beneath its shrink-wrap, you could see that the album art for *Some Girls* was something special. The cover and sleeve were designed by Peter Corriston, who had done the album art for Led Zeppelin's 1975 double-album *Physical Graffiti* and who would go on to design the covers for the Stones' next three albums, *Emotional Rescue*, *Tattoo You*, and *Undercover*, winning a Grammy Award in the category of Best Album Package for *Tattoo You*.

The front cover of *Some Girls* featured a die cut design in which black-and-white faces, embellished with red lips and eyes, and in some cases yellow hair, poke through Fifties-style advertisements for wigs. The cover was divided into four colored lines — blue, red, green, and yellow — each featuring five ads, sorted by line according to price: $6.99, $7.99, $8.99, and $9.99. Closer inspection revealed that some of the ad copy was replaced by the names of the album's songs and that the faces under each wig weren't simply the Stones but also some female celebrities: Lucille

Ball, Farrah Fawcett, Judy Garland, Jayne Mansfield, Marilyn Monroe, and Raquel Welch. The back cover presented three columns of brassiere ads — the pointy Fifties kind that looks as if they could have military applications — into which the song titles and musical credits were embedded (see Figure 5.1).

I remember studying the back cover intently before opening up the album and discovering, in tiny type at

Figure 5.1 *Some Girls* back cover

its left and right edges, the following descriptions of the band's members:

[LEFT-HAND SIDE]: BILL WYMAN — Chic, intelligent, confidante of international society — which she regales with her unusual and exciting parties — Bill lacks only one attribute to be the perfect wife — she just doesn't like men. Never has.

KEITH RICHARDS — The elusive "I vant to be alone" Swede has been hiding from the world for years. A frustrating romance with John Gilbert and the tragic death of Mauritz Stiller, Richards' only real love[,] has turned her into a recluse.

MICK JAGGER — Probably the most successful woman in radio, Mick has been very close to marriage. She has the man, admitted she was very fond of him, but sadly sent him away — she couldn't bear to sacrifice her career.

[RIGHT-HAND SIDE]: RON WOOD — The darling of the dazzling twenties had hordes of men at her feet, panting for her favors. Hollywood insiders insist that her great beauty and popularity made it impossible for any man to make an impression on her. None did.

CHARLIE WATTS — The beautiful and talented showgirl, model and actress hasn't found a man who fits her rigorous specifications for a husband. Says the cautious Watts: "I have no regrets . . . I would rather be lonely than sorry . . ."

Not sure what to make of all that, I unwrapped the album and examined the inner sleeve, each side of which bore four rows of five pictures each (see Figure 5.2). The pictures were indeed celebrity photos: I recognized Marilyn Monroe, Lucille Ball, Jayne Mansfield, Judy Garland, Farrah Fawcett, and Raquel Welch on one side — the side that had been visible through the cutouts in the outer sleeve and bore splashes of

Figure 5.2 *Some Girls*, front side of the original inner sleeve

seemingly drawn-on color, red for lips and Lucille and Raquel's hair, yellow for the other four women's hair, plus the fur of a dog. On the other side, more celebrity women, and on both sides, the faces of the Stones superimposed willy-nilly, as if to illustrate the descriptions on the back cover. Slipping the disc out of the sleeve, I put it onto the turntable and waited as the distinctive ambience of needle and vinyl came through the speakers of my stereo . . .

"Miss You"

Liner Notes: Drums, Charlie Watts; Bass Guitar, Bill Wyman; Electric Guitars, Keith Richards, Ron Wood, Mick Jagger; Electric Piano, Ian "Mac" McLagan; Sax, Mel Collins; Harp, Sugar Blue; Lead Vocal, Mick Jagger; Back-up Vocal, Keith Richards, Ron Wood, Mick Jagger

When I first heard "Miss You," I immediately remembered Roy Carr's dismissal of "Fool to Cry" from the Stones' previous album, *Black and Blue*. I found myself smiling when I heard Jagger reprising that song's falsetto vocals with a vengeance on the opening cut of *Some Girls*. It was hard not to imagine Jagger flipping the bird at Carr and other critics who didn't like "Fool to Cry."

Jagger claimed that he wrote the song "during rehearsals for the El Mocambo gig. I remember that because I was waiting with Billy Preston for everyone in the band to turn up. Billy was playing the kick drum and I was playing the guitar and I wrote 'Miss You'." Christopher Sandford offers a slightly different account in his biography of Keith Richards, claiming that Jagger was prompted to write the song in frustration in the aftermath of Richards's bust in Toronto:

> RSO Records released a statement early the next morning. The label announced it was "withdrawing a seven-million-dollar offer to the Rolling Stones for their recording rights to the USA after protracted negotiations." At this point, Mick slammed the door of his suite and got on the phone to Jerry Hall. Later that night, he started writing a song he called Miss You.

Jagger would insist that the song did not refer to Hall or to any particular woman, telling *Rolling Stone*, "'Miss You' is an emotion, it's not really about a girl. To me, the feeling of longing is what the song is — I don't like to interpret my own fucking songs — but that's what it is."

Written in A minor, the song begins with a catchy guitar riff that will turn out to echo the vocal melody over an insistent "four-on-the-floor" bass drum from Charlie Watts. In the third measure, the snare drum kicks in, and the guitar line is echoed by a harmonica two measures later. The sound is unmistakable if you're listening to the album in the summer of 1978: it's the Stones doing disco.

"Disco was [in the air] when 'Miss You' came around," Ron Wood would later say. "We didn't get together and say, 'Let's make a disco song.' It was a rhythm that was popular and so we made a song like that." According to Charlie Watts, "Miss You" was "heavily influenced by going to the discos. You can hear it in a lot of those 'four on the floor' rhythms and Philadelphia-style drumming." Declaring that "in the 1970s . . . there were some fantastic dance records out," Watts recalls that "Mick and I used to go to discos a lot. A great way to hear a dance record is by listening to it in a dance hall or disco — I used to go to dance halls to look at the drummers when I was a kid." Richards, of course, was more dismissive: "We didn't think much of 'Miss You' when we were doing it," he said later.

> It was "Aah, Mick's been to the disco and has come out humming some other song." It's a result of all the nights Mick spent at Studio 54 and coming up with that beat, that four on the floor. And he said, add the melody to the beat. We just thought we'd put our oar in on Mick wanting to do some disco shit, keep the man happy. But as we got into it, it became quite an interesting beat. And we realized, maybe we've got a quintessential disco thing here. And out of it we got a huge hit. The rest of the album doesn't sound anything like "Miss You."

According to Watts, "Keith went mad, but it sounded great on the dance floor."

The musical context for "Miss You" includes songs like the Village People's "YMCA" (1978), which Watts recalls Jagger singing on their way home from a dance club in Munich after a night at a club, and the more complex songs by Earth, Wind & Fire, which Watts deemed "fabulous." Jagger would insist however, that "Miss You" wasn't *simply* a disco song: "'Miss You' wasn't *disco* disco. Disco records at that time didn't have guitars much, and they all had shimmering string lines and oo-eeoo-ee girls. It was influenced by it, but not it. I like that." The chorus of "Miss You" offers us the Stones' take on disco's "oo-eeoo-ee" via Jagger's falsetto doubling of the song's signature guitar line, and it's both compelling and arch at the same time.

One of the elements that make the song unforgettable is the harmonica work contributed by a street musician named James Whiting, who played under the name "Sugar Blue." Whiting was a 22-year-old from Harlem, who was in Paris subsisting on what he could make playing harmonica in the Paris Metro. Jagger told *Rolling Stone*, "Sandy Whitelaw discovered him playing in the Paris Metro. He's a blues harpist from America, and he plays not only in the subway but also in a club called La Vieille Grille. He's a very strange and talented musician."* Wood would later recall Sugar Blue's playing with admiration: "The thing that blew my mind was what that guy could do, because I play a

---

*   Engineer Chris Kimsey tells the story differently: "Earl McGraw, president of Rolling Stones Records at the time, found him in the metro in Paris — heard him playing and just dragged him in one evening . . . Mick told him what to play, he had that da-da derderderderdaah melody worked out, and Sugar Blue was fantastic."

little harmonica. I know how to suck and bend, blow and bend like Jimmy Reed, but if you gave a harmonica to Sugar Blue, he could play in C, C sharp, C flat, B, A and F, all on the one harmonica. The way he bent it was unreal."

Sugar Blue was one of the few session musicians who played on *Some Girls*. The others were Mel Collins, who had played with King Crimson, on the saxophone and the Faces' keyboardist Ian McLagan on electric piano. The liner notes for "Shattered" list three mystery guests on "percussion" — "1 Moroccan, 1 Jew, 1 Wasp." In his memoir *All the Rage* (2000), McLagan writes that Bad Company's Simon Kirke played congas on the track.

Rolling Stone magazine would laud the Stones for "ditch[ing] the vacuousness of Billy Preston," but in fact Preston inadvertently played a large role in the success of the album by suggesting the bass line that would become a key component of "Miss You," which was the album's first single (see Figure 5.3). The song was mixed as a 45 in New York by Bob Clearmountain, who also helped produce an eight-minute version to be played in discos: it would be the band's first 12-inch single (see Figure 5.4). Some copies of the 12-inch were pressed in pink vinyl. (Mine, alas, has gone the way of all things.) A 7:33 minute version of the song appears on the compilation album *Rarities, 1971–2003*, and the accompanying liner notes tell us that, with Clearmountain's help, "Jagger took the basic tracks and extended them, looping the distinctive bass line

Figure 5.3 "Miss You," 7-inch single

and electric piano figures, then adding ad-libbed guitar crosstalk and the harmonica of Sugar Blue, a Chicago native the Stones discovered playing in a Paris metro station." "Miss You" spent 7 weeks on the UK charts, eventually reached No. 3, but it was a much bigger hit in the US, where it would spend 20 weeks on the charts — longer than any of the band's previous 29 singles — eventually reaching No. 1, the last Stones single to achieve that feat.

Figure 5.4 Miss You 12-inch maxi-single

Jagger and Clearmountain punch up the bass line on the 12-inch, and if you listen to that version you quickly understand how integral the bass line is to the overall effect of the song, even in its shorter version.

Richards, who was frequently dismissive of Wyman's contributions to the band, praised Wyman's work on "Miss You." In an interview with *Melody Maker* in 1979, Richards said:

Bill is leaping ahead. Charlie is so magnificent you expect him to go on getting better, and if it doesn't get better at a session you sorta moan at him, "Why aren't you better than last time 'cos you always are!" Bill tends to go more in cycles, and in the last couple of years I haven't seen him so happy and playing so well. Something like "Miss You" proves it.

Wyman himself credited the much-maligned Billy Preston with the inspiration for the song's bass part:

The idea for the bass lines came from Billy Preston. We'd cut a rough demo a year earlier after a recording session. I'd already gone home and Billy picked up my old bass when they started running through that song. When we finally came to do the tune, the boys said, "Why don't you work around Billy's ideas?" I listened to it, heard that basic run, and took it from there. It took some polishing, but the basic idea was Billy's.

Engineer Charles Kimsey remembers that "'Miss You' took quite a time to come together. Bill needed to go to quite a few clubs before he got that bass line sorted out. But he did sort it out, and bless him, it made that song."

"Miss You" was later covered by the legendary blues singer Etta James on her album *Matriarch of the Blues* (2000); James had opened for the Stones during the 1978 tour. Jagger and Richards would perform the song in 2001 at the "Concert for New York," a benefit for 9/11 victims, and in the 2005 Toronto benefit concert that the Stones put together and headlined to help Toronto recover from the economic problems caused by the SARS epidemic, "Miss You" would turn into a duet featuring Jagger and Justin Timberlake. More than any other song from *Some Girls*, "Miss You" would remain a durable part of the Stones' performance repertoire, featured on many of the Stones' post-1978 tours and concert albums.

"When the Whip Comes Down"

Liner Notes: Drums, Charlie Watts; Bass Guitar, Bill Wyman; Electric Guitars, Ron Wood, Keith Richards, Mick Jagger; Pedal Steel Guitar, Ron Wood; Lead Vocal, Mick Jagger; Back-up Vocal, Ron Wood, Keith Richards, Mick Jagger

The opening drum roll and churning guitars of the album's second track, "When the Whip Comes Down," let us know that we've left the world of "Miss You" and Studio 54 and gone downtown to the Lower East Side and the punk scene at CBGB's.

You might think of "When the Whip Comes Down" as the bastard child of Glen Campbell's 1975 hit "Rhinestone Cowboy" and the Ramones' second single, "53rd and 3rd," which was released in 1976. "Rhinestone Cowboy" was written by Larry Weiss in 1974 and included on his album *Black and Blue Suite*. As a single, the song didn't make the charts, but it did receive airplay on easy listening stations. "I first heard the song on KNX-FM in Los Angeles," Campbell said in a 1975 interview with *Billboard* magazine, and soon afterwards it was brought to his attention by Al Coury at Capitol Records. After Campbell performed the song on a telethon, the programming director of KHJ Radio, Paul Drew, called Capitol to find out if Campbell had recorded it. The pressed records weren't ready yet, so Drew grabbed an acetate of the song and added it to RKO's playlist. The song debuted at #81 in May and became a #1 hit 14 weeks later.

"Rhinestone Cowboy" is a song about trying to get by on the streets of New York, after coming to the city in search of fame and fortune:

I've been walkin' these streets so long
Singin' the same old song
I know every crack in these dirty sidewalks of Broadway
Where hustle's the name of the game
And nice guys get washed away like the snow and the rain.

Campbell's protagonist still dreams of the "things [he'll] do / With a subway token and a dollar tucked inside [his] shoe," even as he admits that there's already been "a load of compromisin'" on the way to his "horizon." The song's upbeat mix and Campbell's sunny voice belie the somberness of its lyrics.

The Ramones' "53rd and 3rd" presents a rather different view of life on the mean streets of New York. The eleventh track on the band's eponymous debut album, the song is set a few blocks north and east of Broadway and Times Square at an intersection that was notorious in the mid-Seventies as a locale for male prostitution. According to journalist Nick Kent, the song is based on the real-life experiences of its author, bassist Dee Dee Ramone, who worked occasionally as a male prostitute in the band's early days. The song's narrator describes himself as "a Green Beret in Viet Nam," who now finds himself "Standing on the street / 53rd and Third / . . . trying' to turn a trick." But turning tricks proves to be difficult when "you're the one they never pick . . . Doesn't it make you sick?" The elliptical lyrics of the song's bridge suggests the aftermath of a killing that takes place after the narrator is called a "sissy":

> Then I took out my razor blade
> Then I did what God forbade
> Now the cops are after me
> But I proved that I'm no sissy.

The bridge, which is half-sung and half-shouted by Dee Dee, breaks the deliberate aural monotony of the song and emphasizes the violence of the lyric. No "Rhinestone Cowboy" optimism to be found here.

"When the Whip Comes Down" also tells a coming-to-New York story: following the advice of his "mama and papa," the song's narrator has left Los Angeles, where he's disparaged as a "fag," for New York, where he can simply be "gay." But his hopes are dashed: "wherever I go they treat me the same." The song's second verse puts him at "53rd and Third," where (like the Ramones' protagonist), he's "learning the ropes . . . learning a trade." Full of sexual innuendo, the song bears out Jagger's embrace of what Bill Janovitz calls "the seedy and sordid side of the blues tradition." Janovitz argues that the song is influenced by Lou Reed's streetwise aura: "Jagger not only works with some specific New York street-hustling subject matter, but also in his unflinching delivery: a droning, speak-singing style over a song that is basically two chords until it reaches the bridge — which is just two more chords." The song's A-Mixolydian drone is thickened by guitar work from Jagger, and Wood later suggested that one of his contributions to the album was actually "giving Mick guitar lessons. I encouraged him to play things like 'Respectable,' 'Lies,' 'When The Whip Comes Down,' all that upbeat, punkie stuff. Mick felt very punky at the time." But Woods himself provides an unexpected touch, some twangy pedal-steel guitar-playing that not only looks ahead to "Far Away Eyes" on Side Two, but also signals that this isn't just the Stones doing punk — it's the Stones *out*-doing punk, or perhaps incorporating the punk sound into their own, layering on sonic nuances that are beyond the ken of all but a few punk and New Wave bands.

Moreover, by bringing together sounds associated with both country and punk, the Stones remind us that country music played a role in the rise of New York punk. CBGB's, the club where Television, the Ramones, Blondie, and the Talking Heads first made their mark, had been renamed CBGB & OMFUG by its owner Hilly Kristal. The initials stand for "Country,

Bluegrass, and Blues, and Other Music for Uplifting Gormandizers," and as Bryan Waterman reminds us in his account of Television's album *Marquee Moon*, the band got Hilly to give them a gig by claiming "that country, bluegrass, and blues is exactly what they play — along with a few originals." Richard Lloyd, who played guitar for Television, later described the band's leader Tom Verlaine telling him about meeting Kristal: "One day Tom came and he said, 'I saw this fucking hick, like up on a stepladder — he's opening a bar, calling it CB or something, GB. Do you want to go up there and we'll talk the guy into letting us play?' I said, 'Yeah, of course.'" As Waterman points out, Lloyd's account makes fun Kristal, portraying him as a "fucking hick," but in fact "the idea that country might be the next big scene wasn't as far-fetched as it would later seem: country had made a decent showing in 1973 at Max's [Kansas City], with acts like Waylon Jennings, Willie Nelson, Graham Parsons, and Charlie Rich all sharing the same stage that welcomed the New York Dolls."

Reviewing *Some Girls* for *Sounds* magazine, Pete Silverton described "When The Whip Comes Down" as "probably the most successful straight-ahead rocker on the album. The three guitars of Keef, Ronnie and Mick shoot their way through in a way I never expected to hear from the Stones again." The song would become a staple on the band's 1978 tour, and Robert Christgau wrote that "When the Whip Comes Down" unexpectedly provided a turning point during the concert he attended at the Capitol Theater in Passaic, New Jersey. Describing himself as "somewhat sick at heart" amidst a crowd that reminded him of a "convention," Christgau noted that the band's rendition of "Star Star," "the throwaway rocker that survives as the most standard Stones standard since *Exile*" had "dropped the Passaic onlookers to their seats." The songs from *Some Girls*, beginning with "Whip," changed all of that: according to Christgau,

> the music lost its mechanical aura — through the next eight selections, seven more from *Some Girls* plus "Love in Vain," it gathered power and conviction. Suddenly Jagger seemed interested in what he was doing. It would be going too far to call it sincerity, but there was an ingenuous enthusiasm to his performance that I'd previously encountered only in a callower version on the early albums.

I found a bootleg recording of that performance on YouTube, and I could hear what Christgau was talking about. The song opens with chunky phase-shifted chords from Richards's guitar — that MXR box of his — followed by two loud smashes from Watts's crash symbol: it's a much more aggressive version than the one on the record, even with the addition of Ian Stewart's piano, which becomes prominent at the end of the song. With Jagger on guitar, Wood is free to let his solos rip as the song progresses. Wood's self-declared contribution to the album seems to have paid off on stage in another way as well. Christgau writes that an important component of the band's renewed intensity was the fact that "the guitar that [Jagger] played on most of these songs contained him physically, kept his hands occupied so that he couldn't go looking for trouble while the band played on. Instead, his restless intensity was channeled through his vocal cords. At least on the new songs, the Stones were doing something new."

"Just My Imagination"

Liner Notes: Drums, Charlie Watts; Bass Guitar, Bill Wyman; Electric Guitar, Keith Richards, Ron Wood, Mick Jagger; Back-up Vocals, Ron Wood, Keith Richards, Mick Jagger

From the new, the Stones turn to the old, borrowed, and blue: a cover of the Temptations' "Just My Imagination." Jagger described the Stones' version as a "continuation" of their version of the Temptations' "Ain't Too Proud to Beg" on *It's Only Rock 'n' Roll*. "I'd always wanted to do that song — originally as a duet with Linda Ronstadt, believe it or not. But instead we just did our version — like an English rock & roll band tuning up on 'Imagination,' which has only two or three chords . . . it's real simple stuff."

Included on the Temptations' 1971 album *Sky's the Limit*, the song had been the third song by the group to reach No. 1 on Billboard's Pop Singles chart, a place it held for two weeks (in addition to three weeks atop the R & B chart). A throwback to the group's Sixties soul sound after its foray into psychedelia, the song was the last single to include both Eddie Kendricks and Paul Williams, two of the founding members of the Temptations: Kendricks would leave the band to pursue his solo career just after recording the song, while Williams would be forced to retire for health reasons.

The group's composer and producer Norman Whitfield had actually written the song two years earlier, but delayed recording it because the group's psychedelically inflected songs such as "Runaway Child, Running Wild," "Psychedelic Shack," "Ball of Confusion (That's What the World Is Today)," and "Cloud Nine" (which won a Grammy) were consistently reaching the Top 20. But when the late 1970 single "Ungena Za Ulimwengu (Unite the World)" failed to reach even the Top 30, Whitfield decided that the time was right for "Just My Imagination." The song's guitar, bass, drums, and percussion tracks were recorded by the Funk Brothers, then the Motown studio band, and an orchestral track featuring members of the Detroit Symphony Orchestra, was added in. Unlike the psychedelic songs, which generally featured lead vocals from all five of the Temptations, "Just My Imagination" features Kendrick on lead vocal, with Paul Williams contributing a solo line during the song's bridge. By the time the recording took place, Kendrick was barely on speaking terms with Otis Williams, whom most observers considered to be the group's leader. When the Temptations performed the song on a live broadcast of the *Ed Sullivan Show* on January 31, 1971, Kendricks was positioned off to the side and barely made eye contact with the rest of the group.

"Just My Imagination" is a song about unrequited love and daydreaming, as the song's narrator imagines himself and his putative lover married, raising a family, and having children. But then he reveals, during the song's chorus, that it was "just my imagination / Running away with me." The song begins with just the kind of "shimmering string lines and oo-eeoo-ee" vocals that Jagger disparagingly associated with disco when describing "Miss You." The song's instrumental arrangement combined with Kendricks's smooth falsetto style gives it a dreamy sound that mitigates the feelings of hurt and longing that the lyrics imply.

Jagger had used falsetto vocals on "Miss You," but there are none to be found on the Stones' version of "Just My Imagination" (listed on the album's cover simply as "Imagination," leading to confusion over the years over whether the song should be referred to by the Temptations' title or as "[Just My] Imagination"). The Stones use a stripped-down, uptempo arrangement that features Richards's MXR phase shifter prominently, along with fuzzed-up guitar chords in the right side of the mix, and twangy guitar lines from Wood on the chorus and solo. Wyman adds a restless walking bass line. As in "When the Whip Comes Down," there's a slight country feel to the song, as if the Stones are determined to pay a curious brand of homage to a variety of different musical influences. As Geoffrey Himes put it, reviewing the album for the *Unicorn Times*, the Stones "illustrate their curious position vis-à-vis black rhythm & blues by decleaning the Temptations' 'Imagination' with enough stray, jagged elements to make their version uncommercial." The net effect of the Stones' approach is to highlight the despair at the core of the song and even suggest a hint of building anger, as their version concludes with an instrumental build-up punctuated by Watts's insistent beating on the high-hat before the fade.

It isn't surprising that the tensions implicit in the Temptations' version of the song should be sharpened and raised to the surface by the Stones, given the troubles that beset the band in 1977 and 1978. Jagger's marriage was breaking up, and Richards's stormy relationship with Anita Pallenberg would soon follow suit. Perhaps to heighten the tension, Jagger altered the lyrics to give the song a New York context: Kendricks sang, "Out of all of the fellas in the world / She belongs to you," but Jagger sings, "And of all the girls in New York / She loves me true." He also removes the reference to the "cozy, little home out in the country" in the Temptations' second verse. "I added the New York reference in the song," Jagger told *Rolling Stone* shortly after the album's release, noting that "the album itself is like that because I was staying in New York part of last year, and when I got to Paris and was writing the words, I was thinking about New York. I wrote the songs in Paris."

In retrospect, there's something uncanny about the Stones' choosing to record "Just My Imagination" for *Some Girls*, a song that marked the fracturing of the Temptations with the departure of Eddie Kendricks and Paul Williams. The lyrics can be read as an allegory of the Stones' situation: the singer's dreams of a happy marriage — a metaphor often used to describe the relationship between Jagger and Richards — prove to be illusory. The acrimonious split between Kendrick and Otis Williams would be replayed by the Stones themselves during the Eighties, when Jagger and Richards would barely be on speaking terms after Jagger's decision to try his hand at a solo career. The difference: the Stones would find a way to regroup and re-invent themselves for the Nineties and beyond.

"Some Girls"

Liner Notes: Drums, Charlie Watts; Bass Guitar, Keith Richards; Electric Guitars, Mick Jagger, Keith Richards, Ron Wood; Harp, Sugar Blue; Synthesizer, Bill Wyman; Acoustic Guitars, Keith Richards, Ron Wood; Lead Vocal, Mick Jagger; Back-up Vocal, Mick Jagger

As soon as the needle hit the fourth cut on the album and Richards's phase-shifted guitar came crunching through the speakers, quickly accompanied by Watts's alternating snare and tom-tom, a bass neck slide that turns out to be Richards's work as well, and then the same blues harp work that animated "Miss You," I was transported back to that afternoon on the Long Island Expressway when I first heard "It's Only Rock 'n' Roll" on the car radio. Even before I heard Jagger's soon-to-be-infamous lyrics, "Some Girls" evoked for me the same louche attitude that had drawn me to the band in the first place. Propelled by Richards's rollicking bass line and Watts's stuttering drum work, the song offers up Jagger's catalogue of girls and their proclivities, beginning in general terms — "Some girls give me money, some girls buy me clothes / Some girls give me jewelry, that I never thought I'd own" — before moving on to characterizations by nationality — "French girls . . . Italian girls . . . American girls . . . English girls" — and then by race and ethnicity.

Describing the genesis of the song to *Rolling Stone*'s Jonathan Cott, Jagger claimed,

> I made most of it up just off the bat. I made it up as I went along. I had another version of the song, but when it came to the take, I sang a completely different version — it was eleven minutes long — and then edited it down. I remember that when I wrote it, it was very funny. 'Cause we were laughing, and the phone was ringing, and I was just sitting in the kitchen and it was just coming out . . . and I thought I could go on forever!

I remember thinking it was all pretty funny myself at the time, but then I was just a junior in high school and most of what I knew about women was still hearsay. I figured it couldn't be true that all "black girls just want to get fucked all night," any more than it was true that all "white girls [are] pretty funny" — I knew quite a few who were pretty much humorless. (And, as it turned out, they didn't think the song was funny at all.)

Jagger claimed that his experience was different: "Most of the girls I've played the song to *like* 'Some Girls,'" he told *Rolling Stone*'s Jonathan Cott. "They think it's funny; black girlfriends of mine just laughed. And I think it's very complimentary about Chinese girls, I think they come off better than English girls. I really like girls an awful lot, and I don't think I'd say anything really nasty about them." He's being more than a little disingenuous, of course. Despite his protests, "Some Girls" does have a nasty edge to it. The final line of the song, a seeming throwaway about Zuma Beach — "Let's go back to Zuma Beach / I'll give you half of everything I own" — is clearly a reference to Bob Dylan's recent, bitter divorce from his wife, Sara, who ended up with the couple's house in Zuma Beach.

Cott suggested to Jagger that the song was a send-up of the Beach Boys' "California Girls," in which the girls are "all turned into a different type of girl, and certainly from another state!" Jagger replied, laughing, "It's a great analogy. But like all analogies it's false." But Cott's idea is a useful heuristic: think of them as New York girls, who have come to the city from all around the world. In his eight-part documentary *New York*, the filmmaker Ric Burns describes New York as a "great city dedicated to a crucial experiment . . . the exhilarating, often harrowing experiment to see whether all the peoples of the world could live together in a single place." The lyrics of "Some Girls" offer a jaundiced, archly comic view of New York's cosmopolitanism, but what makes the song exhilarating — and perhaps a little bit harrowing — is its *sound*: played in the key of A, full of interlocking guitars and tasty solos from Wood, it *sounded* to me the way I thought the Stones should sound. It wasn't the neo-disco of "Miss You" or the quasi-punk of "When the Whip Comes Down." It wasn't the updated soul of "Just My Imagination." It was just the Stones reeling off another leering classic in the tradition of "Under My Thumb," "Let It Bleed," "Brown Sugar," and "It's Only Rock 'n' Roll."

In *Rolling with the Stones*, Bill Wyman lists "Some Girls" among the songs that the Stones played occasionally on the 1978 tour, but I haven't been able to find any corroboration and most commentators suggest that the band chose to omit it, along with "Before They Make Me Run." Years later, however, the Stones would perform "Some Girls" at New York's Beacon Theater during the benefit performances for the Clinton Foundation, which were documented by Martin Scorsese in the film *Shine a Light*. Their rendition of the song would feature Richards playing a hollow-body Gibson, Wood playing slide on a sunburst Stratocaster, and Jagger brandishing a blonde Telecaster tuned to five-string open G.

"Lies"

Liner Notes: Drums, Charlie Watts; Bass Guitar, Bill Wyman; Electric Guitars, Keith Richards, Ron Wood, Mick Jagger; Lead Vocal, Mick Jagger; Back-up Vocal, Mick Jagger

"Some Girls" is such a classic Stones song, immediately unforgettable because of its swaggering guitars, lilting bass, and snide lyrics, that many listeners — myself among them — found "Lies," the song that follows it and closes out the album's first side to be something of a let-down, a somewhat perfunctory uptempo number, offering up competent but ultimately forgettable three-chord rock. Reviewing the album for *Sounds*, Peter Silverton described "Lies" as "a rocker that just doesn't quite make it. The playing — especially the guitars and drums are faultless — but the tune just ain't quite good enough." Charles Saar Murray dismissed it in the *New Musical Express* as "purest filler."

"Lies" is my least favorite song on the album. I tend to agree with Silverton's judgment that the song is a cut below the band's best, but it's hard for me to imagine that the Stones thought of it as "filler." For one thing, the band had a lot of tracks from which to choose by the end of the *Some Girls* sessions, so why would the band choose the last song on Side A as a place to put a song that was intended to be filler? Indeed, Ronnie Wood told *Creem*'s Barbara Charone, "There aren't any filler tracks on this album. The band was most aware of avoiding that. From the start we knew the album was going to be full of strong tracks. Anything slightly dodgy was shelved." Moreover, by placing "Lies" where it is, the band calls attention to the song by breaking the pattern established in the albums after *Exile* of closing out Side A with a ballad: "Angie" on *Goats Head Soup*, "Time Waits for No One" on *It's Only Rock 'n Roll*, and "Memory Motel" on *Black and Blue*.

"Lies" is anything but a ballad: it's a three-minute song with three chords — E, A, and D — and its lyrics excoriate a "dirty jezebel" who tells nothing but "lies." The song makes use of the rhetorical device known as *anaphora*, the repetition of a word or phrase at the beginning of successive verses or clauses:

> Lies, dripping off your mouth like dirt
> Lies, lies in every step you walk
> Lies, whispered sweetly in my ear
> Lies, how do I get out of here?
> Why, why you have to be so cruel?
> Lies, lies, lies I ain't such a fool!

Like "Some Girls," "Lies" was one of the songs that Jagger brought to the sessions. Richards would remember, "'Some Girls' was Mick. 'Lies' too." But where "Some Girls" offers a tongue-in-cheek catalogue of the ways in which women are troublesome, "Lies" dispenses with humor and, for the most part, with sentences. Most of the lines consist of the word "lies" followed by an appositive phrase that makes the idea of lying more vivid. The song is a rant, and Jagger's vocal is buried down in the mix, so that what comes across at first listen is the word "lies" and little else.

The band is pissed off — and not just at women. Jagger and the Stones were clearly getting fed up with all the criticism being launched at them by punks like the Sex Pistols. The journalist Nick Kent asked Jagger during the summer of 1977 about a rumor going around that Johnny Rotten had slammed the door of Malcolm McLaren's Sex Shop in Jagger's face. Jagger dismissed it as a bunch of lies:

> Now this is all total fantasy, complete and utter fantasy. I don't even know where the Sex Shop is . . . Hold on, I vaguely recall, where Let It Rock used to be. There's a lot of clothes shops in the King's Road, dear, and I've seen 'em all come and go. Nobody ever slams the door on me in the King's Road. They all know I'm the only one who's got any money to spend on their crappy cloth, though even I would draw the line on spending money on torn T-shirts!

Wood would later say, "Those punk songs were our message to those boys. We never sat around talking about punk, but you couldn't avoid it. It was on the news all the time with the Sex Pistols and the Clash and all the other punk bands. It was something that was in the air exactly the same way that disco was when 'Miss You' came around." Commenting on *Some Girls* in his autobiography, Keith Richards would attribute the "sense of renewal" that marks the album to the feeling that "we've got to out-punk the punks. Because they can't play, and we can. All they can do is be punks." The interweaving rhythm guitars of Richards, Wood, and Jagger; Wyman's restless bass line; Watts's inventive drumming — these are things that are beyond the ability of bands like the Sex Pistols. It's as if the Stones are saying, "Here, we can just toss this off and still sound better than you lot." On "Lies," the Stones prove that they can indeed *play*, but in the end being accomplished musically isn't enough to raise "Lies" to the pantheon of great Stones songs.

The summer before the *Some Girls* sessions, Jagger famously told Sandy Robertson of *Sounds* magazine, "Keith Richard is the original punk rocker. You can't really out-punk Keith. It's a useless gesture." "Lies" is perhaps the Stones' version of a useless gesture. It's the one song on *Some Girls* where they meet but don't manage to transcend the provocations of the moment.

"Faraway Eyes"

Liner Notes: Drums, Charlie Watts; Bass Guitar, Bill Wyman; Piano, Keith Richards, Mick Jagger; Acoustic Guitar, Keith Richards; Pedal Steel Guitar, Ron Wood; Electric Guitar, Keith Richards; Lead Vocal, Mick Jagger; Back-up Vocal, Ron Wood, Keith Richards, Mick Jagger

Flip the album over to the second side, put down the needle, and suddenly you're about 2,800 miles away from the New York punk rock with which Side A concludes. Ronnie Wood describes "Far Away Eyes" as "a bit of Bakersfield country."

I'll admit that I found it puzzling it first and that I'd often turn the record over and skip ahead to the hard-driving opening riff of "Respectable." I couldn't figure out what this song was doing at the start of Side 2 of *Some Girls*, a song about a hick in Bakersfield, California, stuck among songs that are inspired geographically and musically by New York?

I knew, of course, that it wasn't the Stones' first foray into US country music. In fact, my beloved "Honky Tonk Women," which Jagger and Richards had written in Brazil in late 1968, was inspired by the *gauchos* whom they had met at the ranch where they were staying. It was originally conceived as an acoustic country song. "Mick and I were sitting on the porch of this ranch house," Richards would recall in 2003, "and I started to play, basically fooling around with an old Hank Williams idea." That version of the song would show up as "Country Honk" on *Let It Bleed* (1969). The final track on *Sticky Fingers* (1971), "Wild Horses," was recorded at Muscle Shoals Sound Studio in Alabama in December 1969 and is clearly influenced by country. On one of the song's guitar parts, Richards uses "Nashville tuning," in which the top two strings (E & B) are tuned normally but the bottom four (G, D, A, and E) are replaced by lighter gauge strings that are tuned an octave higher than usual to create a bright, ringing sound. "Wild Horses" appealed to country wunderkind Gram Parsons so much that he received permission to record it with the Flying Burrito Brothers; their version actually appeared the year before *Sticky Fingers* came out. *Exile on Main Street* would feature "Sweet Virginia," which Bill Janovitz has described as "a simple acoustic campfire sing-along, a country ditty [that serves as] perfect beginning to an acoustic-based, country and folk-tinged side of songs."

In retrospect, it's not surprising to find the country influence surfacing in the Stones' music in late 1968. "Country music was in the air in 1968, and the Rolling Stones had to breathe it like everyone else," writes Stephen Davis in *Old Gods Almost Dead*. The Stones' connection to country music became personal when they met Parsons after a Byrds gig in London that year. Parsons had joined the Byrds in early 1968, steering the band away from the psychedelic rock that marked *The Notorious Byrd Brothers* (1968) toward the pure country of *Sweetheart of the Radio* (1968), which the band had originally conceived as a compendium of twentieth-century American musical styles. Parsons left the Byrds to begin hanging out with the Stones, and Richards credits Parsons with teaching him "country music — how it worked." Richards had a longstanding interest in country music; in fact, his first public performance, about eight years earlier, had been a country gig with his friend Michael Ross: "we gravitated to country music and blues, because we could play it just ourselves

. . . We did a school party, somewhere around Bexley, in the gymnasium, sang a lot of country stuff as best we could at the time, with only two guitars and nothing else."

What Parsons taught Richards was "the difference between the Bakersfield style and the Nashville style." Parsons himself was an exponent of the rawer, stripped-down Bakersfield style, which Merle Haggard and Buck Owens had pioneered to satisfy working-class audiences in and around Bakersfield, California, and which still bore the cultural imprint of the Okies who had migrated there during the Depression in search of work. The Bakersfield style featured twangy guitars (often Fender Telecasters) and was a reaction to the overproduced, string-laden sound of recordings from Nashville during that era. Richards recalls that Parsons "played it all on piano — Merle Haggard, 'Sing Me Back Home,' George Jones, Hank Williams. I learned the piano from Gram and started writing songs on it."

It was Jagger, though, who would pen "Far Away Eyes," which was one of the songs that the Stones were rehearsing during the sessions that preceded their ill-fated trip to Toronto in February 1977. (Richards would tell an interviewer after *Some Girls* was released that Jagger used to listen to a lot of Merle Haggard.) Written in the key of F, the song opens with piano chords and acoustic guitar strumming over a bass drum alternating with snare rim shots, joined in the second bar by Wyman's heavy lurching bass and Wood's pedal steel. Jagger pipes up with a kind of countrified rap, delivered in a caricature of an American Southern accent:

I was driving home early Sunday morning through
    Bakersfield
Listening to gospel music on the colored radio station.
And the preacher said, "You know you always have the Lord
    by your side."
And I was so pleased to be informed of this
That I ran twenty red lights in his honor.
Thank you Jesus, thank you Lord.

Like "Some Girls" on Side 1, "Far Away Eyes" adopts an ironic mode, perhaps even more so: the song's protagonist is a comic figure that no one is likely to equate with Jagger himself.

    The second verse, also spoken, introduces "the girl" of the title:

I had an arrangement to meet a girl, and I was kind of late.
And I thought by the time I got there, she'd be off . . .
She'd be off with the nearest truck driver she could find.
Much to my surprise, there she was sittin' in the corner,
A little bleary, worse for wear and tear
Was a girl with far away eyes.

Then, finally, some actual singing, as the song swings into a sing-along chorus reminiscent of "Sweet Virginia," with Richards and Wood joining in on backing vocals:

> So if you're down on your luck,
> And you can't harmonize,
> Find a girl with far away eyes.
> And if you're downright disgusted,
> And life ain't worth a dime,
> Get a girl with far away eyes.

The song bears out Jagger's stance toward American country music, which is less respectful than Richards's:

> I love country music, but I find it hard to take seriously, I also think a lot of country music is sung with the tongue in cheek. The harmonic thing is very different from the blues. It doesn't bend notes in the same way, so I suppose it's very English really. Even though it's been Americanized it feels very close to me, to my roots, so to speak.

The year after *Some Girls* was released, Richards complained about Jagger's vocal on "Far Away Eyes":

> Mick feels the need to get into these caricatures. He's slightly vaudeville in his approach. "Far Away Eyes" is like that. He did it great every time except for the final take. It's good when he does it straight 'cause it's funny enough without doing a pantomime. It's the *sound* version of what he was doing wrong *visually*. When he sings it as a caricature it sounds like it would be great for a show. You expect Mick to walk out in his cowboy duds on an 18-wheeler set [*laughs*]. Or sing it into his CB as part of his skit.

Richards's comments foreshadow the tension that would arise in the Eighties as Jagger began more and more to embrace the idea of show business as the heart of the Rolling Stones' endeavors.

In fact, however, the inclusion of "Far Away Eyes" makes *Some Girls* a more complete document of the Seventies in the United States. As historian Bruce Schulman argues in *The Seventies: The Great Shift in American Society, Culture, and Politics* (2001), "the tides of American life turned" during that decade, as "a booming economy and burgeoning population transformed the South and Southwest" from "an outcast region" to one that "wrested control of national politics, sending the winning candidate to the White House in every election after 1964" — a streak ended by Barack Obama in 2008. What the historian John Egerton called "the southernization of America" would stretch beyond the political arena into American popular culture. Five years before the release of *Some Girls*, the Country Music Association had held its directors' meeting in Manhattan, with New York mayor John Lindsay proclaiming the occasion Country Music Day in the city. Schulman notes that "country music and southern rock, cowboy boots and pork rinds, even Pentecostal churches and Confederate flags appeared throughout the nation . . . The brash free-wheeling boosterism of the Sunbelt South gradually enveloped the nation; by the time of the Los Angeles Olympics and Ronald Reagan's 1984 reelection campaign, it had become the national style."

But not in New York, which maintained its disdain for "redneck" culture. If "Far Away Eyes" bears out Jagger's attitudes toward country music, it also aligns itself with the typical New Yorker's attitude toward Southern mores and religious fervor.

Well the preacher kept right on saying that all I had to do
   was send
Ten dollars to the Church of the Sacred Bleeding Heart of
   Jesus
Located somewhere in Los Angeles, California,
And next week they'd say my prayer on the radio,
And all my dreams would come true.
So I did.
The next week, I got a prayer.
For the girl . . . well, you know what kind of eyes she got.

The exaggerated twang with which Jagger pronounces these words — particularly the outlandish name "Church of the Sacred Bleeding Heart of Jesus" — clues us in to the fact that Jagger is ventriloquizing a stereotype rather than creating a believable character, a stereotype that affirms the superiority of the worldliness associated with New York and the capitals of Europe.

In his account of the Stones' 1978 tour, journalist Chet Flippo suggested that

> what Mick and Keith most wanted, after they realized that they didn't really want to become middle-aged poverty-stricken sharecropping Negroes singing the blues in dirt-poor Mississippi was to become rich and

comfortable Southern gentry. The Stones effectively became a United States rock and roll band in the Southern tradition.

Flippo, I think, overstates his case. The Stones *did* want to become rich and comfortable, but they would never identify with New South rednecks in the way that they had with American black musicians like Muddy Waters.

What they sensed, however, was the growing importance of the Southern demographic not only to American popular culture but also to their own record sales. Moreover, they also realized that the so-called "Southernization of America" was in fact a process in which American culture and Southern culture were meeting one another halfway, something that Egerton also knew: "the Southernization of America" was his subtitle for a study that was entitled *The Americanization of Dixie*. The Stones' 1978 tour would begin in Lakeland, Florida, and include a healthy number of dates at Southern venues, and Flippo's account of the audiences at these concerts tallies with Egerton's analysis. Flippo marveled at the way in which the New South "overdid everything in its enthusiasm to embrace new and fashionable things," including the embrace of dope culture by its young people:

> If you had predicted twenty years ago that Southerners — rich and fashionable Southerners, at that — would rush out to embrace (foreign: German) Mercedes cars and (foreign: Colombian) expensive cocaine and

(foreign: British) Rolling Stones music, you would have been called a foreign faggot or worse. No more. I know Dallas bankers and brokers who are "growing up with the Stones" and whose growing-up pains include elaborate pre-Stones dope-and-alcohol parties and then the actual Stones concert and then the post-Stones-concert party.

Flippo concluded that "rednecks came to finally fuel the Stones' myth of invincibility, of arrogant invincibility that should have been shattered by their initial fey image." "Far Away Eyes" is a nod to those rednecks, even as it maintains a stance of superiority. The Stones, after all, were on stage; the rednecks were paying to be in the audience.

The band recorded "Far Away Eyes" during the fall 1977 sessions, with Wood adding the pedal steel solos and fills the following spring. The song was featured on the 1978 tour, and some of its country styling would seep into other songs on the set list during the tour — an approach that would carry over into later tours. In an interview with *Guitar Player* magazine in 1983, after the release of the album *Still Life* and Hal Ashby's concert film *Let's Spend the Night Together*, both of which document the band's 1981–1982 tour, Richards was asked about some changes to "Imagination" that gave the song a country feel. "That's me and Ron doing the parts together," he replied, "and you get that sustaining thing like that. We aren't using a pull-string or a lot of slide right now, but Ron plays pedal steel, a bit on 'Shattered' and 'Far Away Eyes.' Country music's a part of the way we do that kind of thing, and it comes through even if it's done with straight guitars sort of pulling up against each other."

This sense of togetherness is, in fact, implicit in the album's rendition of "Far Away Eyes"; there's a tension between the redneck rap of the verses and the camaraderie of the sing-along chorus, when Jagger is joined by Richards and Wood, the vocals full, suggesting a hint of gospel. "When you're down on your luck, and you can't harmonize," they sing — and they're recording it at a moment in the band's history when the band *does* seem to be down on its luck, accused of being old farts, future harmonizing threatened by the legal cloud hanging over Richards after the Toronto drug bust.

It's also a moment when Jagger has found a new romance with Jerry Hall, who was born in Texas, the daughter of a truck driver. Interviewing Jagger for the June 29, 1978 issue of *Rolling Stone*, Jonathan Cott suggested that the songs lyrics "make it sound as if this dreamy truck-stop girl from Bakersfield, California is really real." Jagger replied, "Yeah, she's real, she's a real girl," before making a joke out of the comment and then suggesting that the song is "really about driving alone, listening to the radio." Later in the interview, he claims that the girl in "Far Away Eyes" is a "combination," like the girl in "Memory Motel" and, in fact, like "nearly all of the girls in my songs."

The seeming sincerity of the song's chorus is underlined when you compare the final version to an alternate take in which Jagger sings in a reedier voice and is unaccompanied on the chorus: in comparison to the finished version, the irony of the spoken verses carries over into the chorus. The camaraderie of the album version is heightened in the second chorus when "harmonize" turns into "sympathize," as the band reaches out to those in its audience who know what it's like to be "down on your luck." "Far Away Eyes" presents a girl — very different from the women of "Some Girls" and "Respectable" — who's there waiting, who hasn't gone off "with the nearest truck driver she could find." The song's protagonist may be a caricature, but there's something genuinely wistful — and hopeful — in the overall effect of the song.

The band would play "Far Away Eyes" on its *Licks* tour in 2002 and then again during the *Bigger Bang* tour in 2006. It was captured on film in *Shine a Light*, an endearing performance that features Jagger on acoustic guitar, Wood on pedal steel, and Richards fumbling the words to the first chorus, drawing a sidelong glance from a seemingly unamused Jagger. But Richards gets a second chance on the next chorus, when Jagger brings the mike over to him and they look at each other, singing "life ain't worth a dime," Richards's right hand reaching over to hang on Jagger's left shoulder — looking at each other with the affection of an old married couple. But then, when Richards heads off to his own microphone, he fumbles the words again, singing "disgusted" instead of "down on your luck." It's a telling moment, as the camaraderie implicit in the recorded version's chorus is borne out years later on stage.

"Respectable"

Liner Notes: Drums, Charlie Watts; Bass Guitar, Bill Wyman; Electric Guitars, Keith Richards, Ron Wood, Mick Jagger; Vocals, Mick Jagger

"Respectable" begins with a Chuck Berry-style blues boogie vamp in A, with a single guitar alternating between E and F on the fifth string, joined by a drum roll from Watts as it shifts to the D chord. A second guitar joins in when the riff returns to A, but this one has a fuzzed-up punky edge to it. When the riff shifts to the E chord, a twangy lead guitar chimes in with bent notes, then is joined by a second, as Jagger starts up with a trademark drawl: "Well . . . now we're respected in society / We don't worry' bout the things that we used to be . . ." Jagger turns "now" into a two-syllable word — "nuh-ow" — to give it a little added emphasis, with Richards joining in with *his* trademark nasal backing vocals at the word "worry." Jagger continues: "We're talking heroin with the President / 'Yes, it's a problem sir, but it can be bent' . . ." — with Richards chiming in again on "heroin" in what seems like a wicked commentary on his drug predicament.

Jagger insisted in his interview with *Rolling Stone*'s Jonathan Cott that the song was meant to be light-hearted: "I thought it was funny. 'Respectable' really started off as a song in my head about how 'respectable' we as a band were supposed to have become. 'We're' so respectable. As I went along with the singing, I just made things up and fit things in. 'Now we're respected in society . . .' I really meant *us*." Cott had suggested to Jagger that listeners might "take a few of these songs on the new LP as being about your domestic situation." Jagger responded by noting that he does indeed mention "my wife" in "Respectable," but insisted that the song was about the band: "My wife's a very honest person, and the song's not 'about' her."

It's hard, though, not to see in the song's second verse a reference to some of the women in the band's life, as the lyrics shift from first- to second-person narrative:

> Well, you're a pillar of society
> You don't worry about the things that you used to be
> You're a rag trade girl, you're the queen of porn
> You're the easiest lay on the White House lawn.
> Get out of my life . . . don't come back!

It is indeed tempting to think of Bianca Jagger as the target at which these lines are aimed. A few years earlier, Bianca had met President Gerald Ford's bachelor son Jack at the White House. *Time* magazine reported it this way:

> Jack's return to the White House left him with a case of the intellectual bends. As a friend of David Kennedy, the President's ubiquitous young photographer, Jack met Andy Warhol and Bianca Jagger, and made his way onto the New York City pop-celebrity circuit. On one Manhattan jaunt, Jack, Bianca and Kennedy dropped

in at Le Jardin, a discotheque frequented by gays and in-crowd types. Jack later told friends: "I was dancing with Bianca and a fellow came up to me and tapped me on the shoulder and said, 'May I dance?' I thought he wanted to dance with Bianca. He wanted to dance with me!"

Other reviewers suggested that the song was a put-down of Margaret Trudeau.

In the chorus, the song's point-of-view suddenly shifts to the third-person:

> She's so respectable
> She's so respectable
> She's so delectable
> She's so respectable
> Get out of my life
> Go take my wife
> Don't come back!

The first lead break treats us to classic Chuck Berry riffs on top of multiple layered rhythm guitars, before Jagger returns with the chorus. A third verse? Forget about it: interweaving lead guitars return with a vengeance, and the final chorus gives them impression of being shouted as the guitars threaten to drown it out before finally giving way to a classic Watts closing sequence: drum roll, high hat, crash symbol, and a final bass-snare two-beat ending.

"Respectable" was one of the songs that Jagger brought to the studio sessions almost fully hatched in his own head:

With "Respectable" it was all there before we went in, because I like to write the songs that I write as complete as possible. I don't like leaving anything too open. Keith, of course, takes a totally different approach . . . [He likes] to have a lot more open-endedness in his songwriting, which is good in one way but it can be very long-winded. I like to get all the lyrics done before I go in. I don't mind if someone wants to make suggestions to *change* them, because I can do that a lot easier in the studio than write them.

"Respectable" is a rejoinder to all those punks who claimed that the Stones were over the hill in 1977, and Ron Wood would later suggest that "Respectable" and some of the other uptempo numbers from *Some Girls* may well have influenced some of the post-punk indie bands who came later: "Funnily enough, I saw the guys from Green Day backstage on the *Forty Licks* tour: they made some records that reminded me of 'Respectable' and 'When the Whip Comes Down' from *Some Girls*."

The first time I heard "Respectable," I was struck by its driving guitars and breakneck pace, by Jagger's braying — "You're so respectable! . . . Get out of my life, go take my wife . . . Don't come back!" — and by Watts's dynamic drum work. It seemed like classic, kickass, misogynist Stones along the lines of "Brown Sugar" or "Dance Little Sister." (Robert Christgau described it as the kind of song "the Stones hadn't attempted since *Between the Buttons*.") But what struck me on repeated listenings was that first verse with its first-person perspective: "Well . . . now we're respected in society. We don't worry 'bout the things that we used to be." Methinks the band doth protest too much: no matter how punky they try to sound — and as far as I'm concerned "Respectable" *is* a great late-Seventies punk song — the fact remains that in 1978 they are millionaires in their mid-thirties who've been playing rock 'n' roll for about 16 years. For years, interviewers have been asking Jagger just how long he expects to go on "singing in a rock 'n' roll band" now that he's no longer a "poor boy," thank you very much. "Respectable" gets to the heart of the Stones' predicament in the wake of punk: there's something almost "respectable" about their brand of rebelliousness. Call it "luxury rebellion" perhaps; it's a far cry from the grittiness on display on a nightly basis at CBGB's, and the Stones know it. For a brief moment, they're sneering at themselves, before turning their gazes outward. You could argue that "Respectable," like "Some Girls," is an exercise in irony, but in the album's title track, their irony is never pointed in the singer's direction. In "Respectable," for just a moment, we see what turns out to be the future of the Stones, who will reinvent themselves in the late Eighties as a multinational corporation.

Jagger, of course, urged his listeners not to take any of this too seriously, particularly not his lyrics.

> It's very rock & roll. It's not like "Sara." "Respectable' is very lighthearted when you *hear* it. That's why I don't like divorcing the lyrics from the music. 'Cause when you actually hear it sung, it's not what it is, it's the way

we do it . . . "Get out of my life, go take my wife — don't come back" . . . it's not supposed to be taken seriously. If it were a ballad, if I sang it like: "*Pleese*, taaake my wiiii-ife" — you know what I mean — well, it's not that, it's just a shit-kicking, rock & roll number . . . It's whatever works. "Respectable" is light-hearted. So is "Lies." We don't overemotionalize the way we sing them.

In retrospect, however, I think that Jagger was actually being deadly serious in that first verse: *he* doesn't mind being considered "respectable," *he* likes talking to presidents and their ilk, and *he* really isn't "worried 'bout the things that we used to be." That first verse suggests a singer who's interested in embracing change. The problem for the Stones would turn out to be that the rest of the band — and in particular Keith Richards — would continue to cling to "the things that we used to be."

Perhaps predictably, "Respectable" is not among the songs that the Stones play in the film *Shine a Light*, which opens with scenes of the Stones greeting and making non-heroin-related small-talk with President Bill Clinton and his extended family.

"Before They Make Me Run"

Liner Notes: Drums, Charlie Watts; Bass Guitar, Keith Richards; Electric Guitars, Keith Richards, Ron Wood;

Electric Slide Guitar, Ron Wood; Pedal Steel Guitar, Ron Wood; Acoustic Guitar, Keith Richards; Lead Vocal, Keith Richards; Back-up Vocals, Mick Jagger, Ron Wood, Keith Richards. Recorded & mixed by Dave Jordan

If "Respectable" is ultimately Jagger's song, the next cut on the album, "Before They Make Me Run" belongs to Richards. Like *Exile*'s "Happy," it's his chance to sing lead vocal, but the difference between "Happy" and "Before They Make Me Run" is the drug bust that loomed over Richards throughout the making of *Some Girls*. The happy-go-lucky singer of the earlier song, who proclaims, "Never want to be like papa, / Working for the boss ev'ry night and day," is replaced by a world-weary character who's "worked the bars and sideshows along the twilight zone" and discovered what it means to "feel so alone" in a crowd. The protagonist of "Before They Make Me Run" has had his share of "booze and pills and powders" and done his "time in hell": he has more in common with the protagonist of the Ramones' "53rd and 3rd," who also ends up on the run, than he does with the protagonist of "Happy."

It isn't only his lead vocal that makes "Before They Make Run" Richards's song, however: it's the only song on *Some Girls* that is built around the open G tuning that became the guitarist's hallmark. Some of the band's most famous songs get their characteristic "Stones" sound from Richards's use of open G: "Honky Tonk Women," "Brown Sugar," "Can't You Hear Me Knocking," "All Down The Line," and "Start Me Up" all start with open G riffs that can't be duplicated in standard tuning. (And after 1969, Richards has played "Jumping Jack Flash" — arguably the band's signature song, the one song that the Stones have performed on every tour since its release — in open G with a capo at the fourth fret, even though it was originally cut in open D.) For Richards, using open G was a paradigm shift that made him rethink his approach to playing guitar: "Anything you thought you knew has gone out the window . . . You have to rethink your whole thing, as if your piano was turned upside down and the black notes were white and the white notes were black. So you had to retune your mind and fingers as well as the guitar."

Richards credits Ry Cooder with introducing him to open G tuning, though he notes that Cooder "was using it strictly for slide playing and he still had the bottom string." In Cooder's tuning, the bottom string is tuned to D. Richards's innovation was to drop the sixth string so that the new bottom string is tuned to G, the root of the G chord. There's no need then to dampen the bottom string: you can hit it and let it resonate as you play other chords on the rest of the strings and it will still sound right. In his autobiography, Richards waxes poetic about the impact that learning open G had on his playing:

> The beauty, the majesty of the five-string open G tuning for an electric guitar is that you've only got three notes — the other two are repetitions of each other an octave

apart. It's tuned GDGBD. Certain strings run through the whole song, so you get a drone going all the time, and because it's electric they reverberate. Only three notes, but because of these different octaves, it fills the whole gap between bass and top notes with sound. It gives you this beautiful resonance and ring. I found working with open tunings that there's a million places you don't need to put your fingers. The notes are there already. You can leave certain strings wide open. It's finding the space in between that makes open tuning work. And if you're working the right chord, you can hear this other chord going on behind it, which actually you're not playing. It's there. It defies logic. And it's just lying there saying, "Fuck me."

Noting that the sitar works on a similar principle, Richards claims that the "drone" enabled by the use of open tunings connected him not only to "the tribesmen of West Africa," but also to "that meticulous Mozart stuff and Vivaldi," arguing that "they knew that too. They knew when to leave one note just hanging up there where it illegally belongs and let it dangle in the wind and turn a dead body into a living beauty."

Working in open G during sessions that were dominated by songs in the key of A did not, however, make "Before They Make Me Run" an easier song to put together. In fact, it may have made it harder. Richards says that "for sheer longevity — for long distance — there is no track that I know of like 'Before They Make Me Run.' That song, which I sang on that record, was a cry from the heart. But it burned up the personnel like no other. I was in the studio, without leaving, for five days."

Engineer Chris Kimsey recalls that "Keith had a bee in his bonnet about that song. He just wanted to go in and get completely absorbed and lost in it, which he did. He got Dave Jordan in, and I remember seeing Dave after five days in the studio working with Keith on that same song. When he went in he looked quite tanned and healthy; when he came out he was a greyer shade of white. He couldn't handle it after that."

Richards's obsession with getting the song right no doubt stemmed from the fact that it became a focal point for the emotions, worries, and uncertainties of that moment in his life. He himself admits, "It came out of what I had been going through and was still going through with the Canadians. I was telling them what to do. Let me walk out of this goddamn case. When you get a lenient sentence, they say, oh, they let him walk." Richards's reflections on the *Some Girls* sessions in his autobiography, *Life*, are comparatively brief. In fact, journalist Nick Kent notes in his own memoir, *Apathy for the Devil* (2010), that he "sat down one afternoon" with James Fox, the ghostwriter for *Life*, "to share my memories of the great man during his vampire years. Apparently Keith has only the dimmest recollection of what transpired in the Seventies. It figures."

Richards tells us comparatively little about recording the other nine songs on *Some Girls*, other than indicating the importance of the "little green [MXR] box" that he used on a number of songs, and you get the feeling that he still thinks of that album as overly dominated by Jagger's interests. But he goes on at length about "Before They Make Me Run":

> "Why do you keep nagging that song? Nobody likes it." "Wait till it's finished!" Five days without a wink of sleep. I had an engineer called Dave Jordan and I had another engineer, and one of them would flop under the desk and have a few hours' kip and I'd put the other one in and keep going. We all had black eyes by the time it was finished. I don't know what was so difficult about it; it just wasn't quite right. But then you get guys that'll hang with you. You'll be standing there with a guitar around your neck and everybody else is conked out on the floor. Oh no, not another take, Keith please. People brought in food, *pain au chocolat*. Days turned into nights. But you just can't leave it. It's almost there, you're tasting it, it's just not in your mouth. It's like fried bacon and onion, but you haven't eaten it yet, it just smells good.
>
> By the fourth day, Dave looked like he'd been punched in both eyes. And he had to be taken away. "We got it, Dave," and somebody got him a taxi. He disappeared, and when we were finally finished, I fell asleep under the booth, under all of the machinery.

He awoke to discover the studio in use by the members of the Paris police band, managing to escape with his stash undetected.

Richards begins the song high on the guitar's neck, with a double-struck G barre-chord at the 12th fret, followed by a characteristic suspended chord, which adds an E and C to the mix on the fourth and second string respectively, before the riff descends down the neck to hit E-minor, C, and D, and before coming to rest on an open G. In tablature format, it looks something like this:

```
            hammer-on                      slide
D ------12--12--12--12---x ---0 --- 5 ---- 5 -- 7 ---0 ------
B ------12--12--13--12---x ---0 --- 5 ---- 5 -- 7 ---0 ------
G ------12--12--12--12---9 ---0 --- 5 ---- 5 -- 7 ---0 ------
D ------12--12--14--12---9 ---0 --- 5 ---- 5 -- 7 ---0 ------
G ------12--12--12--12---9 ---0 --- 5 ---- 5 -- 7 ---0 ------
D ----------------------------------------------------------
```

The hammered-on chord is played like an augmented A-minor chord in standard tuning. Richards uses this chord over and over again: it provides the two primary hooks in the intro to "Brown Sugar" and it's what makes "Happy" happy, providing the hook in the chorus.

Life in "Before They Make Me Run" is a series of good-byes: whether you're walking or running, you're moving on. The lyric that precedes the first chorus — "Well here's another goodbye to another good friend" — took on additional poignancy when Richards would play the song without Jagger and the Stones during his tours with the X-Pensive Winos. Making a cameo appearance in Richards's autobiography, Waddy Wachtel, the other guitarist in the Winos, relates an anecdote about "Before They Make Me Run" that suggests that the classic intros to so many open G Stones songs are essentially variations on a theme:

We got on stage with the Winos one night and we're about to do "Before They Make Me Run," and he goes to the intro and he starts to hit it and goes . . . "Argh, I don't know which one it is!" Because he has so many introductions that are all based on the same form. The B string and the G string. Or the B string and the D string. He just went, "Which one are we doing, man? I'm lost in a sea of intros." He's got so many of them, a whirling dervish of riffs, open G intros.

In fact, "Before They Make Me Run" was not the only signature open G song to emerge from the *Some Girls* sessions. A tune that Richards had originally taped as a reggae song in 1975 during the *Black and Blue* sessions turned into something else, a straight-ahead rocker in C built around Keith's characteristic suspended chords at the fifth and second frets of the open G guitar. The band had just finished the master for "Miss You." Chris Kimsey recalls, "Throughout the recording, Charlie kept it very straight ahead and Keith just went for it. It was like 'Oh, I remember this,' as they played along, and it just stuck together with a lot of space. That's the song's magic."

But when Richards heard it, he didn't like it, still thinking it was supposed to be a reggae song and worried that it was in fact too close to something he had heard on the radio, but could no longer place. He told Kimsey to wipe it.

Kimsey kept it. Three years later, when he was pulling together previously recorded masters to create the album that would become *Tattoo You*, Kimsey resuscitated the cast-off song and persuaded the band to work on it. It would be the album's first single, reaching No. 2 on the *Billboard* Hot 100 and becoming one of the band's signature numbers. The song was called "Start Me Up."

"Beast of Burden"

Liner Notes: Drums, Charlie Watts; Bass Guitar, Bill Wyman; Electric Guitars, Keith Richards, Ron Wood; Acoustic Guitar, Keith Richards, Ron Wood; Lead Vocal, Mick Jagger; Back-up Vocals, Keith Richards, Mick Jagger

"Beast of Burden" stands out as the one true slow song on *Some Girls* (the relatively slow tempo of "Miss You" being mitigated by its driving four-on-the-floor disco beat). Written in the key of E, the song was a product of Keith Richards's anguish during the early months of 1977 after being convicted of cocaine possession in the UK. In his biography of Richards, Christopher Sandford describes the period in this way:

> He spent the next month shuttling between New York, Paris and finally Redlands. It was never going to be easy for Keith to move back to the Sussex countryside, and kick drugs with a woman who was shooting heroin. The dealers arrived nightly, and on top of that the house

was being watched again. Nor was it easy for Anita: "I suffered a bad bout of depression after the baby died and I wasn't able to cope with [Angela]," she said of that difficult year. Before long, Keith was spending more and more time locked in the Redlands bathroom with his stash and his guitar. With massive aid from his new snorter, he wrote a haunting ballad there called "Beast Of Burden."

Downstairs, the American journalist Barbara Charone was busy researching Keith's authorized biography. The couple she witnessed were heartbreaking in their concern for one another. Also their fury. "I haven't been fucked in months!" Anita screamed one night. "Is television more important than me?"

Richards would later claim that the song was written not with Pallenberg in mind, but rather Mick Jagger:

> When I returned to the fold after "closing down the laboratory," I came back into the studio with Mick, around the time of *Emotional Rescue*, to say, "Thanks, man, for shouldering the burden" — that's why I wrote "Beast of Burden" for him, I realize in retrospect — and the weird thing was that he didn't want to share the burden any more. Mick had grown used to running the show — and I slowly became aware that he resented any interference.

Richards would nevertheless describe "Beast of Burden" as a "collaboration." Jagger detailed the process through which the song took shape in an interview with Sylvie Simmons of *Mojo* magazine:

How it works on a tune like "Beast Of Burden," is Keith would set up a chord sequence and maybe one or two lines, and then you've got to extemporise on that, and come up with these melody lines and lyrics. We just ran the chord sequence through a lot of times — we were open-ended in the studio, so we just tried lots of different ways of doing the beats and the arrangements. The actual chord sequences are the same, but the stuff in there that makes the sections different is the different vocal lines. I would just scat the thing and come up with "pretty prettyprettyprettyprettypretty girl" and all the little talk sequences — I hesitate to use the word 'rap' — and after all this the song is different melodically from the actual original.

The song is a collaboration in another way: more than any other song on the album, it showcases the interweaving guitars of Richards and Wood. Written in the key of E, the song begins with Richards using his MXR phase shifter on the right side of the stereo mix, soon joined by Watts and then Wood on the left side. In comparison to the distorted sounds of "When the Whip Comes Down," "Lies," and "Respectable," the overall sound of "Beast of Burden" is clean, and there's no real lead break, just interweaving guitars playing fills against one another throughout the song, beneath and beside the vocals.

And the vocals are perhaps Jagger's best work on the album, ironic given that he has said that he would have omitted the song if it had been wholly up to him, wanting the album to have only uptempo numbers.

On an earlier take preserved on the bootleg *Girls, Pills, and Powders*, you can hear him experimenting with falsetto vocals in the verse. In the final version, falsetto is limited to the phrases about "pretty girls" and, appropriately enough, about being "tough enough"; in the verse, Jagger uses chest voice, delivering a straight-ahead, no-nonsense performance that is soulful, miles away from the strutting irony of "Some Girls." There's something of the world-weariness of "Before They Make Run" in the lyrics of "Beast of Burden," as the song's protagonist sings, "My back is broad but it's a-hurting" and finds himself puzzled by his lover's standoffishness:

> Yeah, all your sickness I can suck it up
> Throw it all at me I can shrug it off
> There's one thing baby that I don't understand
> You keep on telling me I ain't your kind of man

Lines like these make it hard not to see the song as a comment on Richards's relationship with Pallenberg, though given her comments about their sex life together, it isn't clear which of the two would be the model for the protagonist. Jagger's interpretation for Jonathan Cott of *Rolling Stone* is compellingly nuanced: "'Beast of Burden' is integrated slightly: I don't want a beast of burden. I don't want the kind of woman who's going to drudge for me. The song says: I don't need a beast of burden, and I'm not going to be your beast of burden, either."

But it's also hard not to see the song as another example, along with "Respectable," of the band presenting its ambivalence and uncertainty about its current situation for all to see. Paul Nelson, reviewing the album for *Rolling Stone*, saw in "Beast of Burden" an allegory of the band's predicament in 1978, in which the band's stance of "rebellion . . . lacks a certain credibility, and the cause is simply survival." According to Nelson, "when Mick Jagger implores, 'Ain't I rough enough / Ain't I tough enough / Ain't I rich enough / In love enough / Oooo, ooh please,' he's got to be thinking about himself and the Rolling Stones, among other things. It's too bad the answer to all his questions isn't an unqualified yes. In a better world, it should be."

Other critics, however, were more positive. Reviewing the album for *Sounds*, Peter Silverton called "Beast Of Burden" "a delicate yet muscular ballad which wipes the floor with things like 'Melody' [from *Black and Blue*]." Robert Christgau, who hadn't been particularly impressed by "Beast of Burden" when he first listened to the album, cited the song (in addition to "Love in Vain" and "Shattered") as one of the highlights of the Stones' 1978 concert, writing in *The Village Voice* that these songs "took on a resonance and directness that up to now Jagger has barely played with."

More than ten years after the release of *Some Girls*, after Jagger and Richards had both made solo albums, after the Stones had nearly split up but then reconstituted themselves as a big-time show business band with corporate sponsorship, Tom Wheeler would interview

Richards for *Guitar Player* magazine and ask whether he thought that Curtis Mayfield might have been an influence on "Beast of Burden" and on "Almost Hear You Sigh" from the *Steel Wheels* (1989) album. Richards acknowledged that Wheeler's suggestion was "a very accurate pinpointing of influences," before elaborating on the genesis of the later song:

> When you're playing something like that, the obvious thing you start hitting is the soul licks [*hums a descending, major-scale hammer-on/pull-off line*]. When we first did "Almost Hear You Sigh," I played it very much like "Beast Of Burden." In fact, it was too much like it, so I called it "Cousin Of Beast Of Burden" [laughs]. I didn't know if it was going to get any further than a poor relative. But as we started to add the bridge part and it started to open up for me, then I thought to myself—exactly what you said—Curtis Mayfield. It's that style. Curtis is the king of that.

Although "Almost Hear You Sigh," was nominated for a Grammy and features fine singing and guitar playing, it just isn't in the same league with "Beast of Burden," a fact the Stones themselves have implicitly acknowledged, including the later song in their set lists only on the 1990 Urban Jungle Tour of Europe that followed its release as a single.

"Beast of Burden," meanwhile, would be listed as number 435 on Rolling Stone magazine's list of 500 Greatest Songs of All Time and number 433 on the list of 500 Greatest Rock and Roll Songs of All Time.

Bette Midler included a cover of "Beast of Burden" on her *No Frills* album in 1983; the single version reached #71 on Billboard's Hot 100 Chart. The comic promotional video for the song featured a cameo from Mick Jagger and a frame tale that begins with tabloid headlines — "Bette and Mick?" "Bette Dumps Sheikh for Mick!" "Mick Dumps Everyone for Bette" — followed by Mick's arrival at Bette's dressing room in order to break up with her — Bette: "Listen, just stay long enough to hear me sing your song. I sing it better than anybody." Mick: "Well, *almost* anybody." — only to end up joining her onstage for a rousing rendition of the song and a comic final comeuppance.

Other notable covers would be performed by Buckwheat Zydeco (*Where There's Smoke There's Fire*, 1990), Urban Love + Aneka (on the Australian Bossa Nova compilation *Bossa n' Stones*, 2006), and Los Lonely Boys (*Keep on Giving: Acoustic*, live, 2010). The LA-based alternative band Lifehouse performed the song for the "Stripped" music sessions sponsored by iheartradio.com, saying that they wanted to "pay homage to the godfathers of rock." Perhaps the most insightful cover version is the rendition by the Kooks, an English indie band, who play the song live in a medley with the Velvet Underground's "Sweet Jane," illuminating the two songs' intersecting chord changes. Interestingly, in the summer of 1977, a few months before the Stones would head to Paris for the sessions that would produce the music for *Some Girls*, Mick Jagger told journalist Nick Kent,

Lou Reed started everything about that style of music, the whole sound and the way you play it. I mean, even we've been influenced by The Velvet Underground. No, really. I'll tell you exactly what we pinched from him. Y'know 'Stray Cat Blues'? The whole sound and the way it's paced, we pinched from the first Velvet Underground album. Y'know, the sound on 'Heroin.' Honest to God, we did!

"Shattered"

Liner Notes: Drums, Charlie Watts; Bass Guitar, Ron Wood; Electric Guitar, Keith Richards; Lead Guitar, Ron Wood; Pedal Steel Guitar, Ron Wood; O/D Electric Guitar (in solo), Keith Richards; O/D Tom-Tom, Charlie Watts; O/D Bass Drum, Ron Wood; Lead Vocal, Mick Jagger; Back-up Vocals, Ron Wood Keith Richards, Mick Jagger; Percussion, 1 Moroccan, 1 Jew, 1 Wasp

It all comes together on "Shattered," the album's closing statement, a punk-inflected song with a twanging country bridge that became a staple of dance floors in the summer of 1978. Reviewing the album for *NME*, Charles Shaar Murray argued that "Shattered" was

> the first real Modern Stones track, incorporating flashes of much of what's happened since The Stones last deigned to take any notice of the rest of the rock scene: a thudding robotic beat with menacing deadpan backing vocals and an exuberant Jagger performance that's half JA toasting adapted for a Bowiesque *motorik* beat and

half Patti Smith rants-in-my-pants. The Stones finally meet the New Wave.

Years later, Jagger would remember that "Keith had the riff and this line, 'sha-doobie', and I came up with all the melody and the lyrics, all that stuff about New York, after the track was cut." Jagger's recollection rings true: there are two versions of "Shattered" on the bootleg *Girls, Pills, and Powders*, labeled Takes 1 and 2, without vocals or pedal steel, just Richards's phase-shifted guitar, bass, and drums. In an interview published in the November 1977 issue of *Guitar Player* magazine, Richards noted that even a few years earlier, "pedals and gadgets were just a hassle," but

> now you've got the MXR phasers that can sound so good if they're handled right. I use them onstage for a couple of numbers. I find that it's best if people don't notice them that much. If you overdo it, and everybody realizes that you're using a phaser, then I think you're on the wrong track already.

On "Shattered," however, Richards broke his rule, achieving the song's distinctive guitar sound by using — one might even say flaunting the use of — an MXR phaser — "the 100 model" — and then "damp[ing] the guitar" on the song's basic track. The final version, however, is a dense overlay of live and overdubbed guitar: the tablature included in *The Rolling Stones Guitar Anthology* (published by Hal Leonard Corporation) lists seven different guitar parts.

The song offers a vision of New York City in the late Seventies as a seedy place where "the crime rate's going up upupupup," a city full of vermin — "rats on the West Side / Bedbugs uptown" — and foolish people "chitter-chatter[ing]" about fashion on Seventh Avenue in the Garment District. Jagger uses the Yiddish word *schmatta*, which means "rag" but was used for many years to denote New York's Garment Industry, fueled by Jewish immigrant labor and identified with Manhattan's Seventh Avenue below 42nd Street. The word is occasionally also used taken to mean junk or low-quality merchandise, which also serves Jagger's purpose in the song. Together with the words "shattered" and "shadoobie," the word *schmatta* creates a sonic aura of sibilant menace that is heightened by Jagger's multiple overdubbed vocals over each "shattered" and "shadoobie," as if the lead vocals are being accompanied by a chorus of the undead.

Meanwhile, the lead vocals themselves are surprisingly distinct compared to the slurring that marks classic Stones tunes on *Sticky Fingers* or *Exile on Main Street* and even compared to the rest of *Some Girls*. "With a song like 'Shattered,' Jagger told *Rolling Stone*, "I thought we had to hear the words a bit, so . . . . it's not really just a question of loudness, it has to do with clarity of diction — whether I enunciate properly." In other words, Jagger wants us to listen to these lyrics as words rather than suggestive sounds: he wants us to close the album with the vision of urban decay and psychological unrest that the song describes: "What a mess / This town's in tatters / I've been shattered / My brain's been battered / Splattered all over Manhattan." As in "Far Away Eyes," the lyrics are mostly spoken, but there's no hint of self-directed irony in Jagger's vocal inflection: he's deadly serious, even when he's using jokey slang, and his scorn is turned outward.

Like "When the Whip Comes Down" and "Before They Make Me Run," "Shattered" is a meditation about life on the street and on the run: "pride and joy and dirty dreams and still surviving on the street." The song is also, like "Respectable" and "Some Girls," a meditation on the perils of celebrity, as the singer finds himself surrounded by "money grabbers" and flatterers, and sees New York as a place of "pride and joy and greed and sex." It's a town of people who are hungry for "success, success, success." In other words, the song is a meditation both on what it means to live in New York and what it means to be a Rolling Stone. At the end of the Seventies, for both the city and the band, simply surviving seemed to be the name of the game.

Chapter Six – Aftermath

Almost immediately, *Some Girls* generated controversy.

One week after its release, Atlantic Records was pressuring the band to alter the lyrics to the title song, or at least to the lines "Black girls just want to get fucked all night / I don't have that much jam." New York's premier black music station, WBLS, refused to play "Miss You," because of what it deemed to be the offensive racial attitudes of the album and the band. Ahmet Ertegun, the chairman of Atlantic Records (the US distributor for Rolling Stone Records), tried unsuccessfully to get the station to change its stance.

The controversy deepened when the Reverend Jesse Jackson joined the fray, calling for a boycott of the album. At the time, Jackson was the head of the civil rights organization PUSH (People United to Save Humanity), which had embarked on a campaign in 1976 to have "sexy songs" banned from radio airplay. Jackson met with Ertegun, and afterwards denounced the song as a "racial insult" that "degrades blacks and women." Ertegun commented, "When I first heard the song, I told Mick that it was not going to go down well. Mick assured me that it was a parody of the type of people who hold these attitudes. Mick has great respect for blacks. He owes his whole being, his whole musical career, to black people." Jagger refused to budge, however, telling *Rolling Stone*, "I've always been opposed to censorship of any kind, especially by conglomerates. I've always said, 'If you can't take a joke, it's too fucking bad.'"

Jackson's campaign failed: by the time *Rolling Stone* ran an editorial in November defending the band's right to freedom of expression, the album had already sold more than 4 million copies. Likening Jackson's call for a boycott to the Ku Klux Klan's campaign against "Negro records" in 1955, *Rolling Stone* wrote, "It's naïve to think that a rock & roll song — especially one that is meant only as a parody of feminine stereotypes — could unravel the social fabric . . . Jackson's calls for censorship are abhorrent in a free society." The magazine accused Jackson of simply "seeking to regain a lost power base, and he has seized upon a publicity campaign to purify all pop music — both black and white — as the easiest way to get headlines." Nevertheless, Earl McGrath, the president of Rolling Stones Records, did issue an apology on October 12: "It never occurred to us that our parody of certain stereotypical attitudes would be taken seriously by anyone who heard the entire lyric of the song in question. No insult was intended, and if any was taken we apologize."

Meanwhile, the album art for *Some Girls* soon proved controversial: Lucille Ball, Farrah Fawcett, Liza Minnelli (on behalf of her mother, Judy Garland), the estate of Marilyn Monroe, and Raquel Welch all threatened to sue. On July 5, the WEA plant stopped producing the original inner sleeve, which was replaced by a new sleeve in which the likenesses of all the women depicted in the first edition were removed and replaced by swaths of blue, yellow, and pink, some bearing the inscription "Pardon Our Appearance. Cover Under Reconstruction" (see Figure 6.1).

Figure 6.1 *Some Girls*, revised inner sleeve

The Stones toured in June and July in support of the album, with Bill Graham serving as the tour promoter. Peter Tosh, whose album *Bush Doctor* had been released earlier in the year by Rolling Stone Records, was the opening act on some dates, occasionally joined onstage by Jagger for their cover of the Temptations' "Don't Look Back." When Peter Tosh and his band did not open, the Stones drew on a variety of supporting acts, including Patti Smith, Foreigner, Eddie Money, Kansas, Journey, Southside Johnny and the Asbury Jukes, Van Halen, the Doobie Brothers, the Outlaws, and Santana. Chet Flippo reported in *Rolling Stone* that Jagger had been ambivalent about touring, and the band put the tour together "at the last minute, adding and dropping cities faster than the entourage could count them." In a later piece, Flippo wrote that tour manager Peter Rudge accused him of getting the story wrong, saying that the band had "started planning [the tour] January 2nd in Barbados; we must have had reservations on a hundred small halls." In any case, the tour was a stripped-down affair in comparison to the band's 1975 Tour of the Americas, meaning that the tour embodied the same back-to-basics approach that the band had used to make *Some Girls*. Eight stadium and arena shows were scheduled, with occasional "small dates" in 10,000- to 15,000-seat auditoriums and even cozier venues added despite the opposition of most of the Stone's staff, including Rudge. Eventually, the Stones would play 25 dates.

The tour was a logistical nightmare, but it established a formula of mixing different sized venues that the band would employ frequently on later tours. *Four Flicks*, a DVD compilation of shows from the 2002–2003 Licks Tour, would emphasize this approach, with a disc to a show from each kind of venue — theater, arena, and stadium. According to Bill Wyman, a typical set list for the 1978 tour looked something like this:

1. "Let It Rock"
2. "All Down the Line"
3. "Honky Tonk Women"
4. "Star Star"
5. "When the Whip Comes Down"
6. "Miss You"
7. "Lies"
8. "Beast of Burden"
9. "Just My Imagination (Running Away with Me)"
10. "Respectable"
11. "Far Away Eyes"
12. "Love in Vain"
13. "Shattered"
14. "Tumbling Dice"
15. "Happy"
16. "Sweet Little Sixteen"
17. "Brown Sugar"
18. "Jumpin' Jack Flash"

Most of the shows had no encore, but when the band was moved to provide one, it was generally either

"Satisfaction" or "Street Fighting Man." Wyman's list of "occasional numbers" includes "Some Girls," "Johnny B. Goode," "Fool To Cry," "Memory Motel," "Get Off My Cloud," and "It's Only Rock 'n' Roll," although other commentators suggest that, of the ten songs on *Some Girls* during the tour, both the title track and "Before They Make Me Run" were never performed. Wood and Richards would include "Before They Make Me Run" on the set lists for the New Barbarians Tour on 1979, as the penultimate song before "Jumpin' Jack Flash," and on the recording *Buried Alive: Live in Maryland*, released in 2006, Wood introduces the song by noting, "We never did play this live as the Stones, though Barbarians were sort of kind enough to let it all hang out and do it."

Early in the Some Girls tour, Jagger became ill, but refused to cancel a show in the 2,000-seat Warner Theater in Washington, DC. The concert went well, but the performance ravaged Jagger's voice, and the band's big show in Philadelphia's JFK Stadium two days later was a near disaster, with 90,000 fans booing when the band refused to play an encore. Reviewing that concert and the follow-up two days later at a much smaller venue, New Yorks' Palladium theater, Dave Marsh concluded in *Rolling Stone* that the Stones were "just another good rock band," arguing that "it's no fairer to dismiss them as boring old farts — despite the fact that their show is frequently very dull — than it is to claim that they are still the greatest." The Stones, he claimed, were performing "on a level far below that of their peak tours." Marsh did approve of both the "streamlined" band and the shorter 90-minute set list, suggesting that the two-and-a-half hours that the band regularly played three years earlier had "obliged [Jagger] to take frequent breaks," leading to "the slackest moments of all." Near the end of the review, Marsh had particularly harsh things to say about Jagger's stage outfit, which was perhaps intended to be an ironic take on late-Seventies disco fashion. The standard costume featured a blazer, loud shirt, plastic pants, Italian shoes, and a red golfing cap (see Figure 6.2). Marsh disparaged the outfit in Rolling Stone as "reminiscent of nothing so much as Bob Hope — or Jerry Lewis, in *The Delicate Delinquent*."

Jagger was so incensed by Marsh's concert review and by Paul Nelson's lukewarm review of *Some Girls* that he revoked the tour credentials of *Rolling Stone*'s tour correspondent, Chet Flippo. (Richards and Rudge had both tried to kick Flippo off the tour earlier, but the journalist had managed to talk them out of it.) Flippo reported this exchange:

"Well, Mick, does this mean you want me to leave?"

"Fuckin' right! I've known *Rolling Stone* a long time and gotten on with a few people. I don't trust many people, you know. I trusted *Rolling Stone* and they let me down. I like you and I'm sorry it's you that's here and not those critics. There ain't gonna be no more."

"Does this mean, then, that you're breaking relations?"

Figure 6.2 Mick Jagger at the Fabulous Fox Theater on June 12, 1978 in Atlanta, Georgia. Photo by Tom Hill (WireImage). Used by permission

"Right! No more access. I like you and I'll talk to you but not for *Rolling Stone*. This is goodbye for *Rolling Stone*. I'm sorry it's you that has to suffer for it. Goodbye."

Before long, however, things between the band and the magazine would be patched up. Jann Wenner, the magazine's editor, published his own review of *Some Girls* in September, discussing the album in tandem with Dylan's *Street Legal* and rebutting his own writers. In the first paragraph, he heaps high praise on the album's first single:

> If there's one song that will memorialize this summer, it's "Miss You" by the Rolling Stones. You hear it on the radio almost hourly and everyone in your life seems to be walking down the street to its beat. "Miss You" is an intensely erotic rock & roll ramble that exemplifies the polish, power, and passion of the Stones. It's a track that equals "Tumbling Dice" and "Brown Sugar," and may even set new standards for the band.

Two months later, the magazine was defending the band against Jesse Jackson's charges.

In recent years, the 1978 tour's reputation has improved among aficionados, and not just because of the hazy glow of memory. The King Biscuit Flower Hour recorded several shows for radio broadcasts, and tracks from these were collected in the well-known bootleg *Handsome Girls* (Swinging Pig Records). More recently, eleven tracks from the June 28 show at the Mid-South Coliseum in Memphis and the entire

July 6 show at Detroit's Masonic Hall have been made available online at the Wolfgang's Vault Archive. The compilers of "The Secret History of Some Girls," an online collection of outtakes and live tracks, argue that although the 1978 tour has long been "reputed to be a sloppy mess, the FM broadcasts of the tour tell a different story."

In October 1978, fittingly, the Stones returned to New York, the city that had inspired *Some Girls*, to appear on the fourth season premiere of the hottest — and coolest — show on US network television, *Saturday Night Live*. To watch that episode today (it's available on the *Saturday Night Live: Complete Fourth Season* DVD set) is to enter a time machine and be transported back to the Seventies. The personalities, the haircuts, the clothes, the jokes: it's 1978 with a vengeance.

There's Mayor Koch, delivering the opening monologue, offering deadpan thanks to "the nation": "We here in New York want to tell those of you in other states how much we appreciate what you did for us when we were down and out and needed your help . . . [*audience laughs*] . . . and you came through. We want to say to all of those of you out there, thanks for the loan; you won't be sorry." New York, he claims, is undergoing "a great renaissance," and *Saturday Night Live* has been "one reason" for it — an "insignificant reason," but a reason nonetheless. The monologue then turns into a dialogue, when Koch offers a "certificate of merit" — a folded piece of paper pulled out of his breast pocket — to John Belushi, a "great New Yorker," who grows more and more indignant about his award ("Isn't there a key to the city or something?") and the city and being underpaid by Universal for his work in the film *Animal House*. Ironically, Belushi would leave *Saturday Night Live* at the end of the season to pursue his Hollywood career.

A little later on, Gilda Radner's "Roseanne Roseannadanna" character appears on the "Weekend Update" sketch to deliver a commentary about Studio 54, which turns out mostly to be a commentary about the designer Halston's "big blister" and the importance of wearing "sensible shoes" while dancing at the disco. When Jane Curtin's anchorwoman pushed for more details, Radner replied: "Well, Jane — just between you and me — it's crazy nuts! They got guys dancing with guys . . . girls dancing with girls . . . guys who look like girls dancing with girls who look like guys . . . girls who look like dogs dancing with themselves."

The Stones took part in two sketches before their musical performance. Wearing a white suit, Jagger appeared with Dan Aykroyd in a send-up of Tom Snyder's *Tomorrow* show, goofing on suburban living and men wearing ladies' clothes. Wood and Watts sat at the lunch counter during the Greek diner skit ("Cheeseburger," "cheeseburger," cheeseburger" . . . "No Coke . . . Pepsi."). Wood had several lines of dialogue, trying vainly to get the right amount of pepper from Bill Murray's thick-headed waiter; Watts had a single word — "Yeah" — after being asked whether he was finished eating. Richards was also supposed to appear in a sketch with Belushi, Murray, and band-leader Paul Shaffer, in which he would have a line about needing to cancel an upcoming concert appearance because "I have to get my blood changed," but the sketch was cut after the 7:30 p.m. dress rehearsal because Richards was too wasted to read the cue card. Laraine Newman reportedly said afterward, "It's interesting to be standing there working with someone who's dead."

Breaking the format of the show, which normally featured two songs by the musical guest separated by several skits, the Stones performed three songs in a row: "Beast of Burden," "Respectable," and "Shattered." Jagger was noticeably hoarse after over-rehearsing during the week, though the rough edge of his resulting vocals actually suited the punk sensibility with which he tried to infuse his performance. For "Respectable," Jagger donned a sunburst Stratocaster and accentuated his punk attitude, pushing Ronnie Wood around and flicking his tongue next to Wood's lip and making contact, causing Wood (whose eyes had been closed) to start in surprise. For "Shattered," Jagger removed his white jacket to reveal a ripped red T-shirt adorned with the word "Beast" and a vaguely Satanic representation of a bull, which he proceeded to rip up further, punk-style. He wore a tight satin white sleeve on his right arm and orange warm-up pants that left little about his anatomy below the belt to the imagination.

Saturday Night Live producer Lorne Michaels, a Canadian, spoke at Richards's trial in Toronto later that month. Michaels, writes Richards in his autobiography, "spoke in court about my role as a slinger of hash in the great cultural kitchen. He did a very elegant job of it." Dan Aykroyd, also a Canadian, was on hand to serve as a character witness if necessary. Richards was found guilty, but received a lenient sentence after an appeal by a blind Canadian fan named Rita, whom Richards calls his "blind angel." Richards had heard about this woman hitchhiking to Stones' shows despite her blindness: "The chick was absolutely fearless. I'd heard about her backstage, and the idea of her thumbing in the darkness was too much for me. I hooked her up with the truck drivers, made sure she got a safe lift and made sure she got fed. And when I got busted, she actually found her way to the judge's house and told him this story." The result: Richards was given a suspended sentence, put on a year's probation, and ordered to play a concert for the benefit of the Canadian National Institute for the Blind. Richards performed two shows the following April, featuring both The Rolling Stones and Ron Wood's band, The New Barbarians.

At the end of his generally negative review of the tour dates that he had seen the previous year, Dave Marsh had written in *Rolling Stone* that he had been moved "once" during the two shows:

> After Keith Richards had been flailing away at the crashing chords of "Jumping Jack Flash," the Palladium show's final song, and was sagging from fatigue at its

conclusion, Mick came up and hugged him. It occurred to me then that we might never see this man onstage again and that, however, lackluster it all may be right now, that would be a very great loss.

What Marsh surely could not have imagined is what ended up happening: that Richards and the Stones would play onstage for nearly 30 more years. When the Toronto prosecution's appeal of Richards's sentence was denied in September 1979 by the Ontario Court of Appeal, Richards — and the Stones — were given a new lease on rock 'n' roll life. They would be able to soldier on.

But what the Canadian legal system did not accomplish, the band's own internal dynamics nearly did. Marsh had wondered how the Stones would "cope with the Eighties." The Stones emerged triumphant from the Seventies, but the Eighties nearly did them in. In his memoir, Nick Kent describes *Some Girls* as the band's "last real album of consequence," but notes that

> the record's subsequent success only set into motion yet another long creative slump. By 1979 Jagger and Richards had fallen into open conflict over key issues regarding the group's general direction, and Ronnie Wood was busy introducing himself to the new and extremely costly form of drug dependency then emerging from the West Coast of America: freebase cocaine.

When the Stones did not perform in Europe after the 1978 American tour, breaking a touring pattern that dated back to 1967, Richards went on the road with Wood and the New Barbarians in support of Wood's solo album *Gimme Some Neck* (1979).

Throughout 1979, the Stones worked on tracks for *Emotional Rescue*, their follow-up to *Some Girls*. Released in June 1980, the album was a critical flop, but did well commercially: it was No. 1 on the US charts for seven weeks and gave the band their first UK No. 1 album since *Goat's Head Soup* in 1973. But the sessions for the album hadn't gone well, with tensions arising as Richards, though still hooked on heroin, was nevertheless trying to assert more creative control over the band's music. When it came time to deliver a new album the following year, Richards and Jagger were barely on speaking terms. Engineer Chris Kimsey came to the rescue, putting together a collection of masters left over from studio sessions going as far back as *Goat's Head Soup*. Jagger finished writing lyrics and recorded vocals in Paris in the middle of 1981; Richards only showed up during the mixing sessions in New York later in the year. Defying the odds, the resulting album, *Tattoo You* (1981), would produce two hit singles with "Start Me Up" and "Waiting for a Friend," becoming the band's last album to reach No. 1 on the US charts. Unlike *Emotional Rescue*, *Tattoo You* was also well reviewed by most critics. The tour that followed, once again promoted by Bill Graham and documented by Hal Ashby's film *Let's Spend the Night Together* (1982), set sales records and was the largest grossing tour of the year. The equally successful

European tour that followed in 1982 would turn out to be the last tour by the band for seven years.

Jagger refused to tour behind the Stones' next album *Undercover*, preferring instead to pursue his solo career. In his autobiography, Richards accuses Jagger of treating the band as if they were merely "hirelings": "That had always been his attitude to everyone else, but never to the band. When it dripped over onto us, that was it." Richards describes the atmosphere in the studio during the sessions for the 1986 album *Dirty Work* as "horrendous," noting that "Bill Wyman almost stopped turning up; Charlie flew back home." Richards began writing by himself, producing tracks such as "Had It With You," "One Hit (to the Body)," and "Fight" that were, in retrospect, "full of violence and menace." Richards's continuing bitterness about the fact that Jagger signed a solo deal for three albums without the prior knowledge of the rest of the Stones is palpable in the pages of his autobiography. When Jagger refused again to go on the road with the Stones, preferring instead to tour behind his second solo album, *Primitive Cool* (1987), the period that Richards calls "World War III" began.

Richards, however, would have his revenge, putting together a band, The X-Pensive Winos, and releasing an album, *Talk Is Cheap* (1988), which received glowing reviews, with many reviewers describing it as the best Rolling Stones album since *Some Girls*. His solo tour was also a success, documented on the album and video *Live at the Hollywood Palladium, December 15,*

1988, which included two Stones songs, "Happy" and "Connection."

The Stones, however, would survive "World War III." Unlike the Beatles, whose collaboration lasted barely a decade; unlike the Temptations, who lost founding members after the recording of "Just My Imagination"; and unlike the punk band Television, to whom critics compared the Stones in 1978 (often unfavorably), the Stones would not break up. Jagger and Richards discovered that, professionally at least, they needed not only one another, but also the band known as "The Rolling Stones."

In 1989, the Stones were inducted into the Rock 'n' Roll Hall of Fame along with the Temptations and Stevie Wonder, and one year after the Beach Boys, the Beatles, the Drifters, Bob Dylan, and the Supremes. Jagger had given the induction speech for the Beatles the year before and had closed out the show with a rendition of "Satisfaction," accompanied by a host of others performers, including Bruce Springsteen. A year later, he took the stage with Keith Richards, Ronnie Wood, and Mick Taylor. It was the first time he and Richards had shared a stage in a number of years. Dressed in a shiny black tuxedo-like suit, Jagger quipped, "It's slightly ironic that tonight you see us on our best behavior, but we're being rewarded for 25 years of bad behavior." Not one to shy away from either irony or self-consciousness, Jagger noted an obligation to be "slightly sappy" on such occasions. He proceeded to declare that he was proud not only of having worked "with this group of musicians for 25 years," but also of "the songs that Keith and I have written over the last 25 years," a comment perhaps intended to be a public olive branch to his estranged songwriting partner. After noting the contributions of Ian Stewart and Brian Jones to the band's success, Jagger closed by remarking, "Jean Cocteau said that, 'Americans are funny people. First you shock them, then they put you in a museum.' Well, we're not quite ready to hang up the number yet, so on behalf of the Stones, I'd like to thank you very much for this evening." The finale featured renditions of "Honky Tonk Women" and "Start Me Up," the former featuring Tina Turner on vocals with Jagger amidst a crowd of rock luminaries.

In fact, shortly before the Hall of Fame induction, Jagger and Richards had met in Barbados to begin composing new songs; the rest of the band would join them in Montserrat in the spring to work on the album that would become *Steel Wheels*. The Stones were by no means ready to hang their numbers in the rafters (a ritual that Jagger had no doubt remarked in his visits to sports arenas over the years).

In what seems now like an acknowledgment by the band that they were closing the books on an era in their career, the Stones appeared in a documentary entitled *25 x 5: The Continuing Adventures of the Rolling Stones*, for which *Saturday Night Live*'s Lorne Michaels served as executive producer. The liner notes to the VHS cassette called it "the first time that the Stones have gone on camera to tell their own story" and promised "devastating frank narratives" by members of the band. The concluding minutes of the documentary extol the virtues of rock 'n' roll domesticity, with scenes of Jagger, Jerry Hall, and their children; the weddings of Richards and Patti Hansen, and Wyman and Mandy Smith, whom he had been dating since 1983, when she was 13 years old; and some comments by Charlie Watts on the paradox of needing to be on the road to be a real drummer but preferring to be at home (and going a little stir crazy there). These segments were followed by scenes of the 1989 tour and the band's latest video, "Rock and a Hard Place," featuring concert footage and fireworks, bringing the documentary to a triumphant conclusion.

Bill Wyman's autobiography, *Stone Alone*, published in 1990, offered a similarly optimistic assessment of the state of the band: "The American tour was a vindication of the Stones, and of rock 'n' roll as an enduring art . . . We ended the eighties stunningly, with a degree of band harmony, energy and musical strength stronger than any of us would have dared to predict."

What Wyman didn't know then was that the 1989 tour would be his last with the band. He would announce his decision to leave the Stones in 1992, the year after he split up with Mandy Smith. Jagger and Hall split up in 1999, after it came out that Jagger had fathered a child with a Brazilian model. Watts, however, continued to be happily married, and Richards defied the prognosticators by managing to create a stable and lasting domestic life for himself.

With the *Steel Wheels* tour, the Stones would re-invent themselves in the image that the punks of 1978 had scorned: bad behavior was replaced by professionalism. In a 2002 article for *Fortune* magazine, journalist Andy Serwer would identify 1989 as "the beginning of the modern age of the Rolling Stones." From 1989 to 2002 the band would earn "more than $1.5 billion in gross revenues [from] sales of records, song rights, merchandising, sponsorship money, and touring," making them by "far and away the most successful act in rock today." In 1989, the band accepted an offer from the Canadian rock promoter Michael Cohl to take over the management of the band's tours, rejecting a counter-offer from longtime promoter Bill Graham. In his autobiography, Graham described the mental breakdown that occurred in the aftermath of Jagger's rejection and wrote that "losing the Stones was like watching my favorite lover become a whore."

When the band worked with Graham, the promoter would serve as the tour director: it was his job to enlist local promoters who would then work directly with the venues in each city the band planned to visit. Each local promoter would get a cut of the ticket sales — according to *Fortune* roughly 10–15 percent — and then hand the remainder of the proceeds over to Graham, who would pay the bills and, ultimately, the band. Cohl had a different model in mind. He got the members of Pink Floyd, with whom he was acquainted, to introduce him to the Stones' financial advisor, Prince Rupert Loewenstein, to whom he made his pitch: $40 million for 40 shows — guaranteed. Cohl planned to cut out the middle-men (the local promoters), working with the venues himself, while creating new revenue streams through aggressive merchandizing, luxury ticket packages, and — crucially — corporate sponsorship. All of these streams would be carefully coordinated in order to generate an enterprise that was more than the sum of its parts. After Jagger accepted the deal, Serwer notes that there was an additional wrinkle: "Steel Wheels had to be insured — Lloyd's covered Stones tours — and before the insurer would issue a policy, the band had to take physicals. Keith passed, legend has it, to his own astonishment."

Moreover, as Cohl noted, the band put new emphasis on producing a satisfying stage show, whether the venue was a theater, an arena, or a stadium:

> First and foremost, the show itself was the seminal, watershed point. When you look at what a stadium show was pre-Steel Wheels, it was a bit of a scrim, and a big, wide, flat piece of lumber, and that was it. The band turned a stadium into a theater. It all started with Mick. He simply said, 'We have to fill the end space.' It was complicated to the third power and expensive to the fifth. But it worked.

There was a lot at stake for the Stones at the start of the Steel Wheels Tour, which began officially with a show in Philadelphia at the now-demolished JFK Stadium. The concert was sold out, and police made a number of arrests outside as disgruntled fans without tickets tried to get in. The Stones hit the massive stage with the over-the-top showmanship that would be a hallmark of the tour, accompanied by explosions and a wall of fire as the opening of riff of "Start Me Up" blared from Richards's guitar. Then, two songs later, as the band was chugging through "Shattered," their gigantic half-million-watt sound system went dead. Jagger came out and talked to the crowd. The sound crew, led by Benji Lefevre, who had served as Robert Plant's vocal assistant and effects manager during Led Zeppelin's tours, worked quickly to repair a faulty generator. The band dropped "Shattered" from their set list for the rest of the tour. No need to play songs that might be jinxed.

In the end, Jagger's decision to work with Michael Cohl would prove to be shrewd from a business point of view. Steel Wheels became the highest grossing rock 'n' roll tour at that point in the history of the business, and Cohl would produce every subsequent Stones tour. The Bigger Bang Tour (2005-2007) is the second highest grossing tour ever, the $558,255,524 it earned eclipsed only by U2's 360 Tour in 2011.

Even when they aren't touring, the Stones receive considerable income from the sale of rights to their songs. Like Scarlett O'Hara declaring "I'll never be hungry again," the Stones learned from their dealings with Allen Klein and figured out how to make money from their music — lots of money. A profile in *The New York Times Style Magazine* in December 2010 estimated Jagger's personal fortune to be $310 million and noted that "his beady oversight of the Rolling Stones' financial affairs has, famously, helped make the band one of the richest in rock 'n' roll history. When he is on the road, he has been known to keep a map in his dressing room, indicating the city at which the tour will go into profit." As Serwer put it in the 2002 *Fortune* article,

> Unlike some other groups, the Stones carry no Woodstock-esque, antibusiness baggage. The group has tendrils deep in American business, cutting sponsorship and rights deals with stalwarts like Anheuser-Busch, Microsoft, and Sprint. Remember the old Boston Consulting Group matrix of the four types of businesses? Well, if the Stones were a traditional company, they would be the cash cow.

Serwer's assertion is perhaps a more accurate description of Jagger than it is of Richards, the two of whom have adopted quite different approaches to the *meaning* of the Rolling Stones.

Both Jagger and Richards are well aware that rock stars and bands are forced to create personas for themselves. Andrew Loog Oldham taught them that lesson early on. The difference is that Jagger embraces the idea of persona, not simply as a necessary evil, but rather as an opportunity for creativity. For Richards, however, as he himself puts it, "your persona . . . is like a ball and chain." Jagger seems to have intuited the model of meaning-making with which I began this book, understanding that the "meaning" of the Rolling Stones was always socially constructed, a response to various horizons of expectations among listeners, deejays, record executives, and other musicians. He understood that the meaning of the band would change over time. Jagger's willingness to change — to embrace new sounds like disco and punk during the *Some Girls* sessions, to seek the challenge of a solo career, and later to embrace a new business model for the band's tours — would become a source of tension, putting him at odds with Richards, who seems to expect the Stones to remain true to what they were back in the day. In his autobiography, Richards disparages Jagger for "chasing musical fashion" and for his "compulsion to cultivate buddy relationships with CEOs" — both signs of inauthenticity. Richards (perhaps a little disingenuously) portrays himself as a kind of troubadour who puts the quality of the music above all else and disdains the idea of commercial thinking. "I'm not playing this game," he writes in *Life*. "I'm not in show business. Playing the music is the best that I can do, and I know it's worth a listen." For Richards, the band and its music have an intrinsic *meaning* that should remain unsullied by the vagaries of the marketplace. Making money is nice, Richards would have us believe, but it isn't the point.

* * *

New York City, meanwhile, would make its own comeback from the near-bankruptcy of the Seventies, though it would take time. In his introduction to a volume of essays entitled *New York Calling* (2007), the urbanist Marshall Berman describes the history of the city in the latter part of the twentieth century as a set of assaults:

> The first assault on New York, in the '60s and '70s, had featured a heroin epidemic, an explosion of personal violence, a firestorm of arson, and an almost-bankruptcy. The second round, in the '80s and into the '90s, unveiled a homelessness crisis that put thousands of families out on the streets; a new disease, AIDS, which destroyed thousands more people, especially in the fashion and culture industries, and especially the young and healthy; and a new drug (a product of the Federal "war on drugs"), crack, which ravaged neighborhoods that people had broken their backs to stabilize, generated a whole new array of gangs, and raised the homicide level to twenty-four hundred a year, including many small kids who were killed simply for being there.

At the same time, however, "in the 1970s and '80s, a generation of rappers, writers, and street and subway artists made a cultural breakthrough, and created a verbal and visual language of collective pain, a language that was perfectly attuned to a city in the process of coming apart." For Berman, the graffiti in the subway and the rise of hip-hop as a global musical style were the signs that New York would rise again from the ashes. What Berman refers to as "New York Calling" is "a whole generation of kids" who would find a way to "[break] out of poverty and ghetto isolation and become sophisticated New Yorkers with horizons as wide as the world . . . [T]hese kids from the Bronx could tell the world not only that 'We come from ruins, but we are not ruined,' but 'We come from ruins, but we shall overcome."

By the time I returned to the city to teach at NYU in 1993, the area around Washington Square was on the upswing. During the previous decade, living conditions in New York were an obstacle that had to be overcome whenever NYU tried to hire professors, and most faculty members who did agree to come to the university wanted to live in the suburbs or in Brooklyn Heights. By the early Nineties, however, NYU had a housing crunch, because more and more faculty members wanted to live in downtown Manhattan. Republican mayor Rudolph Giuliani had begun to tackle the problem of crime in the city, and his aggressive policies seemed to work. In an essay entitled "New York State of Crime," novelist TimMcLoughlin confesses

> to being among the early Giuliani supporters at the time of his election. We had had enough, and it was time to fight back. Rudy's quality-of-life initiatives seemed silly, but cleaning graffiti, fixing broken windows, and getting rid of squeegee guys actually did create an impression that crime — or street crimes at any rate — were no longer encouraged through municipal neglect.

During Giuliani's administration, the murder rate dropped to its lowest level in 30 years. Giuliani sought to close down, or at least severely rein in, sex shops and topless bars, requiring stores that sold pornography to limit such materials to one-third of their stock and prohibiting topless bars from being any closer than 500 feet from residential housing. As a result, the Times Square of my youth was transformed, quite literally Disneyfied.

There were costs to all this cleaning up, of course. The civil rights of minorities were often trampled on, sometimes viciously, as in the case of Abner Louima who was beaten and tortured in a police precinct in 1997. Louima ultimately won an $8.75 million settlement from the city. Other costs are subtler, as Brian Berger, the co-editor of *New York Calling*, points out:

> New York's erstwhile recovery has had its costs. Successive economic booms — Wall Street, Dot.Com, Wall Street again — Real Estate *and* Wall Street — have all conspired to tame previously feral parts of Manhattan: Hell's Kitchen, the Lower East Side, even parts of Harlem.

Berger's co-editor, Berman, laments the closing of CBGB's in 2006, finding little comfort in Patti Smith's declaration that for the new generation, "The Internet is their CBGB."

In 2001, New York was assaulted again, all at once and in an unprecedented way, and the city suffered horribly during 9/11 and its aftermath. Six years later, however, Berman could describe New York with optimism, in large part because of what he calls its "sexy" multiculturalism. Compared to the Seventies and Eighties, Berman writes,

New York is a very different place today. It has gone through spectacular population growth; the Census Department expects it to reach nine million within a couple of years. It is more saturated with immigrants, more ethnically diverse and multicultural, than it has ever been, more like a microcosm of the whole world — and thanks to New York's distinctively configured public space, you can see this whole world right out there on the streets.

Writing in the *New Yorker* earlier that year about talk of Giuliani's successor Michael Bloomberg's running for the Presidency, cultural critic Adam Gopnik marveled at the changes that had taken place in the city in a few short years:

What makes the idea of ascending from City Hall to the White House possible is the transformation of New York in the past twenty years — one of the largest civic transformations in American history, and certainly the most unexpected. (Theories credit everything from bright new waves of immigrants to grim forced marches of incarceration, and the sociologists can't decide which is right.)

Gopnik noted that it was "hard for people who don't know what the city was like in the seventies or the early eighties to understand not only how different it seemed then but how tragically insoluble its problems were believed to be." The "transformation" of the city, however, has in Gopnik's eyes come at a steep cost: "For the first time in Manhattan's history, it has no bohemian frontier. Another bookstore closes, another theatre becomes a condo, another soulful place becomes a sealed residence. These are small things, but they are the small things that the city's soul clings to."

One of the great fears that gripped New Yorkers when the financial downturn of 2008 hit the city was a return to the bad old days of the Seventies. But out of the troubles of those years came some pretty great rock 'n' roll.

*   *   *

In 2003, *Some Girls* was listed as number 269 on *Rolling Stone* magazine's list of the 500 Greatest Albums of all time.

*   *   *

In 2005, the novelist Michael Cunningham published *Specimen Days*, a novel comprised of three linked stories from New York's past, present, and future. In the third section, the novel imagines Manhattan turned into a theme park, where visitors pay to experience the thrill of being mugged in Central Park. The muggers are played by androids.

*   *   *

In 2010, the Rolling Stones were enshrined in a board game, with the release of "Monopoly: The Rolling Stones Collector's Edition" (see Figure 6.3). You move

Figure 6.3 *Rolling Stones Monopoly* game board

your piece chronologically through the band's career starting with *Beggars Banquet*, taking the place of Baltic Avenue and represented by the originally proposed graffiti and toilet cover, and ending up at *Shine a Light*, which takes the place of Boardwalk. Your travels around the board follow the logic of the band's increasing net worth rather the artistic quality of its albums.

Some Girls is one of the orange properties, located where St. James Avenue would be on the standard Monopoly board.

Chapter Seven – Coda

I didn't get to see the Stones live until 1989, when I managed to catch one of the band's shows at Foxborough, Massachusetts. We had floor seats, which meant that we stood for the Stones' entire set. The concert film that came out of that tour, *Live at the Max*, turned out to be my wife's and my first movie date.

More than a decade later I would return to the same theater on Broadway and 68th Street to see Martin Scorsese's Rolling Stones concert documentary, *Shine a Light*. The film had been shot two years earlier just up Broadway at the Beacon Theater by an all-star team of cameramen. Later that night, I blogged about watching the film:

> It's more than just a filmed concert: it's a concert reimagined through the cinematic imagination of a filmmaker who happens to be a life-long Stones fan.
>
> The craggy faces, hands, and instruments of the Stones fill the screen in extreme close-up, and they look great, wrinkles and all. The cameras struggle to keep up

with Jagger as he careens about the stage. Every now and then, the camera lingers for a moment on Keith's or Ronnie's fingers and guitar, and the riff that's being played jumps out of the soundtrack for an added shot of presence. The film's editing is kinetic, and Scorsese manages to capture the pure joy of being the Stones on stage. The film isn't about trying to understand who the Stones are; it's about representing the larger-than-life selves into which they transform themselves when they're playing live. And in IMAX, they're larger-than-larger-than life.

The film shows us the late-model Stones at their best: they've gotten tighter on stage with age, and I've often entertained the heretical notion that the Stones sound better with Darryl Jones on bass than they did with Bill Wyman. And there are three terrific guest appearances: a worshipful Jack White singing "Lovin' Cup" with Mick; Buddy Guy inspiring worship from none other than Keith on "Champagne and Reefer"; and Christina Aguilera injecting a growling jolt of sexual energy into her duet with Mick on "Live With Me."

The Stones no longer "matter" in the way that they did back in the day, when they seemed to be dangerous countercultural voices, and their last album, *A Bigger Bang*, was entertaining but not nearly as significant as, say, *The Rising* by Bruce Springsteen. The Stones are an oldies band these days, but for my money they're still "the greatest rock 'n' roll band in the world."

Scorsese caught the band during two marvelous shows in an intimate venue, but if you'd been there you wouldn't have gotten to see what you see in *Shine a Light*. You need the light that Scorsese's cameras shine on the band for that.

If you're a Stones fan, a Scorsese fan, or a fan of concert films, make sure to get uptown and see it in IMAX. It may only be rock 'n' roll, but chances are you'll like it.

* * *

Working on this book has put me in mind of another of my high school teachers, one who was very, very different from M. Bolduc. In contrast to the dapper *professeur* who taught me French, my ninth-grade English teacher Mr. Lombardo was (I realize now) a relatively young guy, grungy and long-haired, a real physical presence in the classroom. He had a permanently hoarse voice. I think most of the high school girls that he taught had crushes on him at one point or another. He used to provoke us in different ways to get us to think (as we might say today) outside of the box. He introduced our reading of Shakespeare's *Henry IV, Part I*, for example, by asking us to insult one another publicly in class. It was a gamble — it produced some genuinely uncomfortable moments — but ultimately it made us realize how quickly our insults became lame as we ran out of things to say. And then he let us read Prince Hal and Falstaff going at one another in Shakespeare's play, taking insulting and punning to levels we could not previously have imagined.

On my final report card, Mr. Lombardo concluded his comment with an italicized comment: "*Be more salacious. Burn Athens and go to Istanbul.*" This comment puzzled my very proper Asian mother, but I knew what he meant. Shortly thereafter, inspired both by Mr. Lombardo and "Honky Tonk Women," I would give up playing classical piano and teach myself to play the guitar.

One day, shortly after my English class's exercise in public insulting, one of our class wits made a very funny, but rude comment, a pun directed at one of our classmates just before class was scheduled to begin. I don't remember what the comment was nor at whom it was directed, but I do remember this: one of the girls in the class blurted out, "Nick, that wasn't very *nice*!" Mr. Lombardo looked up, with a devilish look on his face, and said, "You're, right, it wasn't very *nice*. But it *was* . . . good — very, very good."

The Rolling Stones have never, ever been nice, either musically or personally. Read accounts like Barbara Charone's *Keith Richards* (1982), or Stephen Davis' *Old Gods Almost Dead* (2001), Nick Kent's *Apathy for the Devil* (2010), or even Keith Richards's *Life* (2010), and you'll quickly understand what I mean. Listen to Kent, who knows whereof he speaks:

> Probably all big rock acts have a personal trail of destruction stacking up behind them but the one shadowing the Rolling Stones is the biggest of them all, with corpses and broken spirits strewn far and wide across the universe mostly because the victims let their imaginations get too enflamed by what they heard and saw whilst in the group's orbit.

Kent counts himself lucky to have "stared into their dark vortex at close quarters and lived to tell the tale(s) with all my powers of recall still intact."

Moreover, from the standpoint of an ethicist, you'd have a hard time calling the Stones "good." But if you mean "good" as in "adept, expert, practiced, proficient, or skillful" — well, that's a different matter.

Once upon a time — before they transformed themselves into the multi-billion-dollar corporate conglomerate that they are today — they made music that was very, very good. The band produced a string of albums that captured — and slyly commented on — the turbulent cultural dynamics of the Sixties and Seventies. *Some Girls* is the last of those.

Listen to it, and remember.

Appendix

Outtakes

The *Some Girls* sessions produced an unparalleled number of outtakes and half-finished songs, many of which began circulating on bootleg tapes shortly after the 1978 sessions were completed. Bill Wyman later recalled,

> We had such a great time in the studio that we never stopped really. We were going to be there for four or five weeks originally — middle of October till early December — and we were still there in February. We were enjoying ourselves, we were getting things done and getting off on new songs. We probably finished 12 or 13 songs, and then there's a whole mass of demos and jams. We finished up with 96 reels of tape, where a normal band might use six for an album.

The most famous of the tracks that didn't make it onto *Some Girls* is "Start Me Up," which became the signature song of *Tattoo You* two years later. That album would also include "Black Limousine" and "Hang Fire," which the band had recorded at Pathé-Marconi.

My favorite compilation of outtakes and unreleased tracks from the *Some Girls* sessions is called *Girls, Pills, and Powders*, a five-CD collection released in 2003 by Pignose Records (PGN-023) that contains 76 tracks. It includes alternate takes of each of the tracks that ended up on *Some Girls*, versions of songs that would later appear as B-sides (for example, "Everything Is Turning to Gold" and "So Young") or on *Tattoo You* and some tracks that have never been officially released. The collection has been posted online by fans in both FLAC and MP3 formats. Also of interest are the online compilations posted at *The Secret History of Some Girls: The Best of the Rolling Stones' 1978 Archives* (somegirls.posterous.com), which offer the equivalent of three compact discs. The first two collections, *Spare Parts — Unused Songs '78–'79* and *Some People Tell Me — Rhythm & Blues*, offer outtakes from the *Some Girls* sessions but not alternate versions of the released songs; the third collection is culled from FM broadcasts of the 1978 US tour, approximating the standard set list used by the band each night.

Listening to the outtakes gives you a fuller picture of what the band was up to in the studio. There are a number of country songs, the most notable of which is "Do You Think I Really Care?" (also known as "Yellow Cab"). Lacking the ironic posturing of "Far Away Eyes," the song features Wood on pedal steel guitar, along with some twangy Telecaster guitars (probably

set to the bridge pickup) and appealing piano fills, as
Jagger sings about hailing a cab and ignoring a girl:

> Do you think I could ever care
> About a girl, who's almost never there?
> Do you think about the clothes she wears?
> Would change her mind, or turn my hair
> I saw her on the freeway
> I saw her on the E Train
> Saw her hangin' out
> On 52nd & Broadway
> I saw her on the highway
> I saw her on the skyway
> Aw, need a Yellow Cab, Ronnie
> Let me get out of the rain

"The Way She Held Me Tight" (also known as "Misty
Roads") blends together honky-tonk piano, fuzzed-up
guitars, falsetto crooning, and slurred lyrics that hint
at sex and drugs to create a song that feels like a cousin
to "Let It Bleed." Other unreleased (and to my mind
less interesting) country songs include "No Spare
Parts," about a broken family in Texas and "A Different
Kind," a ballad in an early stage of development, with
lots of pedal steel and few words. The instrumental
"Munich Hilton," named after the hotel where guitarists auditioning for the band in the wake of Mick
Taylor's departure were put up, is a country-inflected
song that bears a family resemblance to "Start Me Up,"
marked by twangy guitars with nary a punk influence
to be found.

My favorite of the unreleased straight-ahead rockers is "Fiji Jim" (sometimes referred to as "Fiji Gin" or "Come and Bring Your Electric Guitar"), which serves up a swinging bass line over a boogie beat and brings to mind the *Exile*-era Stones of the early Seventies. Jagger slurs the lyrics nobly as he sings about a guitar player who plays hard and parties harder:

Better watch out for Fiji Jim, come-up and spend the day
Come on and bring your wah-wah pedal, then let's go on
    stage
Ronnie brought about, 50,000 kids, and then slipped out in
    the rain
Fell from the beat to the 25th floor, white girls go insane . . .
. . .
I bust two ribs, you bust 2 arms, his legs is like stumps in
    the rain
His brain is shred, his nose is bled, but his hands, they sure
    could play.

"I Need You" is a piano-driven rocker in which Jagger and Richards trade vocals. "So Young" is hard-edged blues-rock with a down home feel about the attractions of under-aged girls; the song would eventually appear, with reworked lyrics, on CD maxi-singles that accompanied the album *Voodoo Lounge* (1994): it was the third track on the UK maxi-single release of "Love Is Strong" and the fourth track on the US maxi-single of "Out of Tears."

Still unreleased is "Claudine," inspired by the singer Claudine Longet who was arrested for fatally shooting her boyfriend, former Olympic skier "Spider" Sabich, and convicted of misdemeanor negligent homicide. The band worried about being sued for libel. Ian McLagan describes hearing the song for the first time during the *Some Girls* sessions:

> Keith was keen to play me some of the tracks they already had on tape. He put on "'Claudine." The whole band was in classic form, but Mick's live vocal floored me. At the end of the song, he asks the question, "Am I in my right mind to be locked up with these people?" My answer would be "Yes!" It was my favorite band playing at their peak, and although it was never released, Keith gave me a cassette copy that night which I treasure to this day.

The song has an old-time rock 'n' roll feel to it reminiscent of tracks from the band's earliest albums.

Not surprisingly, the Stones played a lot of blues in the studio as they worked to find their groove. In additional to a number of instrumental tracks, there's a compelling song called "Sweet Home Chicago," not a cover of Robert Johnson's signature tune but rather an original that features Richards's MXR effects box front and center. "Petrol Gang" features Ian Stewart on boogie-woogie piano and offers a wry commentary on the oil crisis of the late Seventies: "Please Mr. President, say it isn't so / I don't wanna, pay $10.00 for gas / . . . / I don't wanna sell my Cadillac / I just paid for it."

Bibliography

[K] indicates that a Kindle version is available.

Works by the Rolling Stones

Official Albums and Films, 1969–1989

[Listed in chronological order]

The Stones in the Park, documentary film, September 1969.
  Dir. Leslie Woodhead. Documents the free concert held in
  Hyde Park on July 5, 1969 two days after the death of Brian
  Jones.
Through the Past, Darkly (Big Hits, Vol. 2), compilation,
  September 1969. Prod. Various. Dedicated to the memory
  of Brian Jones. US and UK versions differ.
Let It Bleed, December 1969. Prod. Jimmy Miller.
Get YerYa-Ya's Out, live album, September 1970. Prod. The
  Rolling Stones and Glyn Johns. Recorded during the 1969
  tour in New York and Baltimore. Overdubbed and edited.
Stone Age, compilation, April 1971. Prod. Andrew Loog
  Oldham. UK only.

Sticky Fingers, studio album, April 1971. Prod. Jimmy Miller.

Gimme Shelter, compilation, August 1971. Prod. Andrew Loog Holdham and Jimmy Miller. UK only.

Hot Rocks, 1964–1971, compilation, January 1972. Prod. Various. US compilation, not released in Europe until 1990.

Exile on Main St., studio album, May 1972. Prod. Jimmy Miller. The album was remastered and rereleased in May 2010 with a bonus disc of outtakes and alternate takes.

Rock 'n' Rolling Stones, compilation, October 1972. Prod. Andrew Loog Oldham. UK only. Chuck Berry covers and Berry-related tracks.

More Hot Rocks (Big Hits and Fazed Cookies), compilation, December 1972. Prod. Various. US compilation that includes UK LP tracks and flip-sides. Not issued in Europe until 1990.

Goat's Head Soup, studio album, August 1973. Prod. Jimmy Miller. The initial US pressings contained a censored version of "Star Star."

No Stone Unturned, compilation, October 1973. UK only. B-sides, EP tracks, and one previously US-only track.

It's Only Rock 'n' Roll, studio album, October 1974. Prod. Glimmer Twins. First album with "Glimmer Twins" production credit.

Metamorphosis, compilation, June 1975. Prod. Various. Compilation of outtakes from the ABKO years. US and UK versions differ.

Made in the Shade, compilation, June 1975. Prod. Various.

Rolled Gold, compilation, November 1975. Prod. Various. UK only. Re-released on CD in 2007.

Black and Blue, studio album, April 1976. Prod. Glimmer Twins. Cover pictures Ron Wood as a member of the band.

Love You Live, live album, September 1977. Sides 1, 2 and 4 recorded primarily in Paris, 1976 (with some uncredited sites edited in); Side 3 recorded at the El Mocambo, Toronto, March 1977.

Get Stoned: 30 Greatest Hits, 30 Original Tracks, compilation, October 1977. UK only.

Some Girls, studio album, June 1978. Prod. Glimmer Twins.

Time Waits For No One: Anthology 1971–1977, compilation, June 1979. UK only. Prod. Glimmer Twins and Jimmy Miller.

Emotional Rescue, studio album, June 1980. Prod. Glimmer Twins and Chris Kimsey.

Solid Rock, compilation, October 1980. Prod. Various. UK only. Decca compilation of songs from 1963–1969.

Slow Rollers, compilation, January 1981. Prod. Various. UK only. Final Decca compilation; consists of ballads from 1964–1969.

Sucking in the Seventies, compilation, March 1981. Prod. Glimmer Twins. Contains the album version of "Shattered;" remaining tracks are single edits, a B-side ("Everything Is Turning to Gold"), a live version of "When the Whip Comes Down, "and the previously unreleased "If I Was a Dancer (Dance, Pt. 2)."

Tattoo You, studio album, August 1981. Prod. Glimmer Twins.

Still Life (American Concert 1981), live album, June 1982. Prod. Glimmer Twins. Recorded on the 1981 US tour: November 5–6, 25; December 13, 18–19 December 1981, overdubs: March–April 1982

Story of the Stones, compilation, November 1982. UK only.

Let's Spend the Night Together, concert film, February 1983 (US). Dir. Hal Ashby. Recorded in Tempe, Arizona (December 13 1981) and East Rutherford, New Jersey (November 5 and 6, 1981).

Undercover, studio album, November 1983. Prod. Glimmer Twins and Chris Kimsey.

Rewind, compilation, June 1984. LP. US and UK versions differ.

Video Rewind, video compilation, 1984. Dir. Julien Temple.
    Includes "Miss You" and "Start Me Up," directed by
    Michael Lindsay-Hogg. Conceived by Bill Wyman, who
    (with Mick Jagger) introduces video clips.
Dirty Work, studio album, March 1986. Prod. Steve Lillywhite
    and Glimmer Twins.
Rewind, compilation, December 1986. CD. Adds
    "Heartbreaker" and "It's Only Rock 'n' Roll" to the US LP
    version.
The London Years, compilation, August 1989. Three CDs.
    Singles and flip-sides released by Decca/ABKO.
Steel Wheels, studio album, August 1989. Prod. Chris Kimsey
    and Glimmer Twins.
25x5: The Continuing Adventures of the Rolling Stones,
    documentary film, 1989. Dir. Nigel Finch.

Official Albums and Films with Live or
Alternate Versions of Songs from *Some Girls*

[Listed in Chronological Order]

Sucking in the Seventies, compilation, March 1981. Prod.
    Glimmer Twins. Contains a live version of "When the
    Whip Comes Down" recorded at the Detroit Masonic
    Temple on July 6, 1978.
Still Life (American Concert 1981), live album, June 1982.
    Prod. Glimmer Twins. Includes "Shattered" and "Just My
    Imagination."
Let's Spend the Night Together, concert film, February 1983
    (US). Dir. Hal Ashby.Recorded in Tempe, Arizona
    (December 13, 1981) and East Rutherford, New Jersey
    (November 5 and 6, 1981). Includes versions of "Shattered"
    (Tempe), "Just My Imagination" (Tempe), "Beast of

Burden" (Tempe), and "Miss You" (East Rutherford,
November 6).

Video Rewind, video compilation, 1984. Dir. Julien Temple.
Includes a portion of the "Miss You" video directed by
Michael Lindsay-Hogg.

Flashpoint, live album, April 1991. Prod. Chris Kimsey and
Glimmer Twins. Recorded November 25 and December
19, 1989; February 16 and July 28, 1990; and January 7–11,
1991. Includes "Miss You."

Voodoo Lounge, television concert film, 1998. Dir. David Mallet.
Filmed at Joe Robbie Stadium, Miami, Florida. Features a
9:25 version of "Miss You."

The Rolling Stones: Bridges to Babylon Tour, '97–98, television
concert film, December 1997. Filmed in St. Louis, MO.
Includes "Miss You."

No Security, live album, November 1998. Prod. Glimmer
Twins. Recorded on the 1997–1998 Bridges to Babylon
Tour and features a version of "Respectable." The band
supported the album with a tour of North American arenas
and smaller venues.

The Concert for New York City, film and album, October
20, 2001. Benefit concert organized by Paul McCartney
in response to the 9/11 attacks. Mick Jagger and Keith
Richards performed "Salt of the Earth" and "Miss You"; the
latter was included on the CD.

Toronto Rocks, television documentary film, 2003. Dir. David
Russell. Documents a concert held on July 30, 2003 at
Downsview Park, Toronto, ON, Canada and headlined by
the Stones, who had proposed it to help Toronto's economy
after the SARS outbreak. Proceeds went to charity. Among
the songs the Stones performed was "Miss You," on which
they were joined by Justin Timberlake.

Live Licks, live album, November 2004. Prod. Don Was and
Glimmer Twins. Recorded on the 2002–2003 Licks Tour

and features live versions of "Beast of Burden" and "When the Whip Comes Down."

Four Flicks, 4-DVD compilation, 2004. Documents the 2002–2003 Licks World Tour. Disc 1 includes "Beast of Burden," recorded on November 4, 2002 at the Wiltern Theatre, Los Angeles. Disc 2, recorded January 18, 2003 at Madison Square Garden, New York, includes "When the Whip Comes Down," performed on the set's "B-stage." Disc 3, documenting a stadium show at Twickenham Stadium, London, on August 24, 2003, contains no material from *Some Girls*. The final disc, recorded at the Olympic Theater in Paris on July 11, 2003, includes versions of "Before They Make Me Run" and "Respectable."

Rarities, 1971–2003, CD compilation, November 2005. Contains a the 12-inch dance version of "Miss You" and a live version of "Beast of Burden" (recorded in Los Angeles in 1981) that was original released as a B-side to "Going to a Go-Go," a track from the 1982 live album, *Still Life*. The cover features a still from the video for "Respectable," directed by Michael Lindsay-Hogg, with Bill Wyman edited out.

Buried Alive: Live in Maryland, live album, October 2006. Recorded in 1979 by The New Barbarians featuring Ron Wood and Keith Richards, joined by Stanley Clarke (bass), Ian McLagan (keyboards), Bobby Keys (saxophone), and Joseph ZigabooModeliste(drums). Features "Before They Make Me Run" (Richards on lead vocal), as well as "Love in Vain," "Honky Tonk Women," and "Jumpin' Jack Flash" (with Wood on lead vocal).

The Biggest Bang, 4-DVD compilation, 2007. Dir. Hamish Hamilton, Joe DeOliveira, Anthony Green, Toru Uehara, Mr. Wang Xianshen. Documents the 2005–2006 Bigger Bang Tour. Disc 1, filmed in Zilker Park, Austin, Texas, includes no songs from *Some Girls*; Disc 2, filmed on

Copacabana Beach in Rio de Janeiro, Brazil, includes a version of "Miss You;" Disc 3 includes a version of "Miss You" filmed at River Plate Stadium, Buenos Aires, Argentina, while Disc 4 presents *Salt of the Earth*, a documentary of the tour. An abridged version, featuring the Austin concert, the documentary, and an excerpt from a concert at Saitama, Japan, was released on Blu-ray in 2009.

Shine a Light, documentary film and live album, April 2008. Film dir. Martin Scorsese. Album prod. Glimmer Twins and Bob Clearmountain. Recorded on October 29 and November 1, 2006 at the Beacon Theater in New York. Songs from *Some Girls*: "Shattered," "Some Girls" "(Just My) Imagination," "Far Away Eyes."

Keith Richards and the X-Pensive Winos, *Live and Wicked 1992*, concert film, 2009. Documents the 1992–1993 X-Pensive Winos tour and features a version of "Before They Make Me Run."

Notable Bootlegs and Unauthorized Recordings

1978 Tour Highlights. A compilation of King Biscuit Flower Hour recordings. Online: somegirls.posterous.com.

Girls, Pills and Powders. Pignose Records. Five CDs, outtakes from the *Some Girls* sessions.

New York Palladium. Exile Records. Recorded live in at the Palladium Theater in New York, June 19, 1978.

No Flash, No Gimmicks! Halcyon Records. Recorded live at Will Rogers Auditorium, Fort Worth, Texas, July 18, 1978. The same concert is available as *Handsome Girls*, Swingin' Pig Records.

Out On Bail 1978. Vinyl Gang Productions. Recorded live at the Capitol Theater, Passaic, New Jersey, June 14, 1978.

Pearls At Swine, 1978 Woodstock Rehearsals. Turn On The Run

Records. Recorded Live at Bearsville Studios, Woodstock, NY, USA — May 19, 1978.

Some People Tell Me — Rhythm & Blues. Studio outtakes. Online: somegirls.posterous.com.

Spare Parts: Unused Songs, '78-'79. Studio outtakes. Online: somegirls.posterous.com.

Books

Richards, Keith, with James Fox. *Life*. New York: Little, Brown, 2010. [K]

Wood, Ronnie. *Ronnie*. London: Macmillan, 2007.

Wyman, Bill. *Stone Alone: The Story of a Rock 'n' Roll Band*. New York: Viking, 1990.

— with Richard Havers. *Rolling with the Stones*. New York: DK Publishing, 2002. Richly illustrated with items from Wyman's collection of memorabilia.

Interviews

Cott, Jonathan. "Mick Jagger: The King Bee Talks about Rock's Longest Running Soap Opera," *Rolling Stone* (29 June 1978).

Dalton, David, and Mick Farren, eds. *Rolling Stones: In Their Own Words*. London: Omnibus Press, 1995.

Heller, Zoë. "Mick without Moss." *Times Style Magazine* (5 December 2010).

Holland, Jools, and Dora Lowenstein, eds. *The Rolling Stones: A Life on the Road*. New York: Penguin Studio, 1998.

Loewenstein, Dora, and Philip Dodd, with Charlie Watts, eds. *According to the Rolling Stones: Mick Jagger, Keith Richards, Charlie Watts, Ronnie Wood*. San Francisco, CA: Chronicle, 2003. Contains a useful chronology and discography.

Miles, comp. *Mick Jagger: In His Own Words*. London: Omnibus Press, 1982.

Paytress, Mark. *The Rolling Stones Off the Record: Outrageous Opinions and Unrehearsed Interviews*. 2nd edn. London: Omnibus Press, 2005.

Remnick, David. "Groovin' High: The Life and Lures of Keith Richards." *New Yorker* (1 November 2010).

Sexton, Paul. "At Home with Keith Richards." Radio Interview. BBC2. Broadcast 28 December 2010.

Welch, Chris. "An Outlaw at The Ritz: Keith Richards." *Melody Maker* (13 January 1979).

Wenner, Jann. "Mick Jagger" and "Keith Richards." *The Rolling Stone Interviews*. New York: Little, Brown. 2007. [K]

Sheet Music Anthologies and Tablature

The Rolling Stones Anthology. Colgems-EMI, 1990. Piano versions. Includes all of *Some Girls*.

The Rolling Stones Guitar Anthology. Milwaukee, WI: Hal Leonard, n.d. Includes guitar notation for several songs discussed in this book, including the following from *Some Girls:* "Beast of Burden," "Miss You," "Respectable," "Shattered," "When the Whip Comes Down"

www.ultimate-guitar.com/tabs/rolling_stones_tabs.htm

BOOKS ABOUT THE ROLLING STONES

Appleford, Steve. *The Rolling Stones: The Stories Behind Their Biggest Songs*. 1997. London: Carlton Books, 2010.

Bockris, Victor. *Keith Richards: The Biography*. New York: Da Capo, 2003. [K]

Booth, Stanley. *The True Adventures of the Rolling Stones*. London: Heinemann, 1985. [K]

Carr, Roy. *The Rolling Stones: An Illustrated Record*. New York: Harmony Books, 1976.

Charone, Barbara. *Keith Richards: Life as a Rolling Stone*. 2nd edn. New York: Doubleday, 1982.

Clayson, Alan. *The Rolling Stones: The Origin of the Species: How, Why, and Where It All Began*. New Malden, Surrey, UK: Chrome Dreams, 2007. [K]

Crampton, Luke, Tim Lister, and Dafydd Rees, eds. *Rock Diary: The Rolling Stones*. Original Media, 2009. [K]

Dalton, David. *The Rolling Stones: The First Twenty Years*. New York: Knopf, 1981.

Davis, Stephen. *Old Gods Almost Dead: The 40-Year Odyssey of the Rolling Stones*. New York: Broadway, 2001. [K]

Flippo, Chet. *On the Road with the Rolling Stones: 20 Years of Lipstick, Handcuffs, and Chemicals*. New York: Doubleday, 1985.

German, Bill. *Under Their Thumb: How a Nice Boy from Brooklyn Got Mixed Up with the Rolling Stones (and Lived to Tell About It)*. New York: Villard, 2009. [K]

Giuliano, Geoffrey. *The Rolling Stones Album: Thirty Years of Music and Memorabilia*. New York: Viking, 1993.

Greenfield, Robert. *Exile on Main St.: A Season in Hell with the Rolling Stones*. New York: Da Capo, 2006. [K]

—*S.T.P.: A Journey Through America With The Rolling Stones*. New York: Saturday Review Press, 1974. [K]

Hill, Susan. *The Rolling Stones: Unseen Archives*. New York: Barnes and Noble, 2004. Charts the band's career through photographs from the archive of the *Daily Mail*.

Janovitz, Bill. *Exile on Main Street*. New York: Continuum, 2005.

Kent, Nick. *Apathy for the Devil: A Seventies Memoir*. New York: Da Capo, 2010. [K]

Norman, Philip. *The Stones*. 1984. Rev. edn. New York: Penguin, 1993.

Richardson, Perry ed. *The Early Stones: Legendary Photographs of a Band in the Making, 1963–1973*. New York: Hyperion, 1992. Photographs by Michael Cooper; foreword and commentary by Keith Richards; text by Terry Southern.

Sandford, Christopher. *Keith Richards: Satisfaction*. New York: Carroll & Graf, 2003.

—*Mick Jagger: Primitive Cool*. New York: St. Martin's, 1993.

Seay, David. *Mick Jagger: The Story Behind the Rolling Stone*. New York: Carol Publishing Group, 1993.

Articles, Essays, and Reviews

Bosso, Joseph. "Keith! Tunings, Teles, and the Cosmic Shuffle: The Rolling Stone Goes Solo." *Guitar World* (December 1988).

Buskin, Richard. "Classic Tracks: 'Start Me Up,'" *Sound on Sound* (April 2004).

Charone, Barbara. "Keith and the Cockroaches: Rip This Joint," *Creem* (June 1977).

—"Keith Richard: Exile On The 32nd Floor." *Sounds* (2 April 1977).

—"Keith Richard: One Man's Week Off the Hook," *Sounds* (22 January 1977).

—"Rolling Stones." *Creem* (January 1978).

—"The Rolling Stones: Glimmer Twins Held Responsible." *Creem* (July 1978).

Christgau, Robert. "The Rolling Stones." *The Rolling Stone Illustrated History of Rock 'n' Roll*. Jim Miller, ed. 1976. Rev. edn. Anthony DeCurtis and James Henke, with Holly

George-Warren. New York Random House: 1992: pp. 238–51.

—"The Stones in 1978." Village Voice (10 July 1978).

Cott, Jonathan. "The Rolling Stone Interview: Mick Jagger: The King Bee Talks about Rock's Longest Running Soap Opera." Rolling Stone (29 June 1978): pp. 42–7.

Cromer, Ben. "For Producer/Engineer Chris Kimsey, Things Got Rolling with the Stones." Billboard (6 May 1995): p. 68.

DiLorenzo, Kris. "The Rolling Stones." Grooves (January 1979).

Flippo, Chet. "Nothing Lasts Forever." Rolling Stone (21 August 1980): pp. 38–42, 52.

—"Rolling Stones Gather Momentum." Rolling Stone (27 July 1978): pp. 8, 21–2.

—"Shattered." Rolling Stone (7 September 1978): pp. 10–14.

Himes, Geoffrey. "Stones Still Hungry After All These Years." Unicorn Times (1 July 1978).

Kent, Nick. "Mick Jagger Hits Out At Everything In Sight!" NME (15 October 1977).

—"The Rolling Stones: Love You Live" NME (24 September 1977).

Kutina, Scott. "Keith Richard." Guitar Player (November 1977).

Marsh, Dave. "The Stones: Just Another Rock Band?" Rolling Stone (10 August 1978): p. 68.

Murray, Charles Shaar "The Rolling Stones: Some Girls." NME (10 June 1978).

Nelson, Paul. "The Guys' Can't Help It; Some Girls, The Rolling Stones" Rolling Stone (10 August 1978): pp. 51–3.

Peck, Abe, "Stones Lyric Protest," Rolling Stone (16 November 1978): p. 39.

Serwer, Andy. "The Rolling Stones: Inside Rock's Billion-Dollar Band," Fortune (30 September 2002).

Silverton, Peter. "The Rolling Stones: *Some Girls*." *Sounds* (10 June 1978).

Simmons, Sylvie. "Rolling Stones: Shattered." *Mojo* (October 2002).

Snowden, Don. "The Rolling Stones: Love You Live." *Rock Around The World*(November 1977).

Swartley, Ariel. "The Rolling Stones: What Kind of 'Rescue' is This?" *Rolling Stone* (21 August 1980): pp. 45–7.

Tosches, Nick. "Stones Rise from the Dead: *Some Girls*, The Rolling Stones." *Circus* (14 September 1978): 73.

Welch, Chris. "An Outlaw At The Ritz: Keith Richards," *Melody Maker* (13 January 1979).

Wheeler, Tom. "Keith Richards." *Guitar Player* (April 1983).

—"Keith Richards: Not Fade Away." *Guitar Player* (December 1989)

Documentary Films

25 × 5: The Continuing Adventures of the Rolling Stones. Dir. Nigel Finch. 1989.

Cocksucker Blues. Dir. Robert Frank. 1972.

Gimme Shelter. Dir. Albert Maysles, David Maysles, and Charlotte Zwerin. 1970.

Stones in Exile. Dir. Stephen Kijak. 2010.

Websites

www.Allmusic.com. See especially Bill Janovitz's short pieces about tracks from *Some Girls*.

patell.org ("Cyrus R. K. Patell's Website"). Includes the entry
"Shining Light" (http://patell.org/2008/04/shining-light/).
www.rollingstones.com. The band's official website.
"The Secret History of Some Girls": somegirls.posterous.com
www.timeisonourside.com/chron1977.html
www.wolfgangsvault.com. A repository of classic live
performances and interviews. Among the concerts by the
Stones are two from the 1978 tour: Memphis (June 28),
which features "Miss You," "Shattered," "Respectable,"
"Beast of Burden," and "When the Whip Comes Down;"
and Detroit (July 6), which features "Lies," "Miss You,"
"Beast of Burden," "Just My Imagination," and "Shattered."

Historical and Musical Contexts:
Articles, Books, and Videos

Anonymous, "The Nation: Arson for Hate and Profit," *Time*
(31 October 1977).
—"The Nation: Jack Ford: 'My Turn to Sacrifice.'" *Time* (20
October 1975).
Berger, Brian. "Public Spaces." In *New York Calling: From
Blackout to Bloomberg*. Marshall Berman and Brian Berger,
eds. London: Reaktion Books, 2007.
Berman, Marshall. "Introduction." In *New York Calling: From
Blackout to Bloomberg*. Marshall Berman and Brian Berger,
eds. London: Reaktion Books, 2007.
Blashill, Pat, et al. "The 500 Greatest Albums of All Time."
Rolling Stone (11 December 2003): pp. 83–178.
Burns, Ric, and James Sanders with Lisa Ades. *New York: An
Illustrated History*. New York: Knopf, 1999.
Crandall, Bill, et al. "The 500 Greatest Songs of All Time."
Rolling Stone (9 December 2004): pp. 65–165.

Cunningham, Michael. *Specimen Days*. New York: Farrar, Straus, Giroux, 2005.

Egerton, John. *The Americanization of Dixie: The Southernization of America*. New York: Harper's Magazine Press, 1974.

Gold, Mick. "Patti Smith: Patti in Excelsis Deo." *Street Life* (29 May 1976).

Gopnik, Adam, "Gothamitis." *The New Yorker* (8 January 2007), pp. 21–2.

Gould, Jonathan. *Can't Buy Me Love: The Beatles, Britain, and America*. New York: Three Rivers Press, 2007. [K]

Graham, Bill and Robert Greenfield. *Bill Graham Presents: My Life Inside Rock and Out*. 1992. Rev. edn. New York: Da Capo, 2004. [K]

Haden-Guest, Anthony. *The Last Party: Studio 54, Disco, and the Culture of the Night*. New York: HarperCollins, 2009.

Kent, Nick. "Never Mind The Sex Pistols, Here Comes The Wrath Of Sid!" *NME* (17 December 1977).

Kozak, Roman. *This Ain't No Disco: The Story of CBGB*. Boston: Faber and Faber, 1988.

Lankevich, George J. *New York City: A Short History*. New York: NYU Press, 2002.

Levin, Mark, dir. *Schmatta: Rags to Riches to Rags (We Have Come Full Circle)*. Blowback Productions / HBO. 2009. Documentary about the New York garment industry.

Logan, Andy. "Around City Hall: Friends in Need," *New Yorker* (15 August 1977).

Mahler, Jonathan. *Ladies and Gentleman, the Bronx Is Burning: 1977, Baseball, Politics, and the Battle for the Soul of a City*. New York: Farrar, Straus, Giroux, 2005.

Marsh, Dave. *Glory Days: Bruce Springsteen in the 1980s*. New York: Pantheon Books, 1987.

—"Punk, Inc.," *Rolling Stone* (29 December 1977).

Martin, Linda, and Kerry Segrave.*Anti-Rock: The Opposition to Rock 'n' Roll*. New York: Da Capo, 1993.

McLagan, Ian. *All the Rage: A Riotous Romp Through Rock and Roll History*. New York: Billboard Books, 2000.

McLoughlin, Tim. "New York State of Crime." In *New York Calling: From Blackout to Bloomberg*. Marshall Berman and Brian Berger, eds. London: Reaktion Books, 2007.

McNeil, Legs, and Gillian McCain. *Please Kill Me: The Uncensored Oral History of Punk*. 1996. Rev. edn. New York: Grove, 2006.

Punk Magazine 16 (March–April 1979).

Saturday Night Live: The Complete Fourth Season. Seven DVDs. 2008.

Schulman, Bruce J. *The Seventies: The Great Shift in American Culture, Society, and Politics*. New York: Free Press, 2001. [K]

Smith, Patti. *Just Kids*. New York: HarperCollins, 2010.

Warhol, Andy. *The Andy Warhol Diaries*. Pat Hackett, ed. New York: Random House, 1991. [K]

Waterman, Bryan. *Television's Marquee Moon*. New York: Continuum, 2011.

Cultural Theory

Greenblatt, Stephen. "Culture." In Frank Lentricchia and Tom McLaughlin, eds. *Critical Terms for Literary Study*. 1990. 2nd edn. Chicago, IL: University of Chicago Press, 1995.

Jauss, Hans Robert. "Literary History as a Challenge to Literary Theory." In Timothy Bahti, trans. *Toward an Aesthetic of Reception*. Minneapolis, MN: University of Minnesota Press, 1982.

Williams, Raymond. *Marxism and Literature*. New York: Oxford, 1977.

Also available in the series: